AF424476

SHIELDING SHADOWS

ABHISHEK KUMAR

Copyright Page
SHIELDING SHADOWS
Copyright © 2025 by Abhishek Kumar

crafting a fictional narrative. The story does not intend to reveal or speculate on actual strategies, locations, or operational details of any nation's armed forces or intelligence agencies.

No classified information or real-life military data has been used in the writing of this book. The portrayal of the Line of Control (LoC), army bases, air force stations, and cross-border issues is entirely fictional and does not reflect any official stance, strategy, or plan of any government or military establishment.

This book is meant for entertainment purposes only and is not intended to defame, discredit, or misrepresent any country, religion, organization, or individual.

For information, contact:
Abhishek Kumar
abhishekkumar.work01@gmail.com
First edition
ISBN:
Cover design by: Madhuri Batham
Edited by: Ms. Supriya

When you go home tell them of us and say,

"For your tomorrow, we gave our today"

-Kargil War Memorial

Preface

In the unforgiving theatre of conflict, truth is often the first casualty. What seems like terror on the surface may conceal layers of deception far more sinister than the bombs and bullets that follow. This is the story of Zunaid, a gentle, bright-eyed boy who lost everything in a terrorist attack, his parents, his home, and the very meaning of childhood.

Left adrift in a world that offered no answers, Zunaid was easy prey for those who sought to mold his grief into a weapon. He was reborn as Omar, a name whispered with fear, forged in the fires of hatred and vengeance. Indoctrinated by a ruthless terrorist organization, he rose quickly, planning what would have been one of the deadliest attacks on Indian soil. But what Omar believed to be justice, what he believed to be a mission of vengeance, was only a pawn's role in a much larger game.

This novel is not just a tale of terrorism. It is a tragic descent into manipulation, betrayal, and the erasure of a boy's soul. It is a mirror to the harsh realities of war, where even the most monstrous face may hide a heart that once knew love, laughter, and loss.

Zunaid's story — Omar's fate — is a reminder that in the wars we see, there are often wars we don't.

Acknowledgement

This novel, though fictional, is rooted in the harsh realities of terrorism and the human cost it carries. At its core, it is a tribute to the valiant men and women of the Indian Armed Forces and Intelligence Services. Their tireless efforts, courage under fire, and unwavering commitment to national security have inspired this story. It is because of their vigilance that many real-life threats are neutralized before they can unfold. To them, I offer my deepest respect and gratitude.

I would also like to extend heartfelt thanks to my parents, my sister and my wife whose constant support, encouragement, and patience carried me through the long hours of writing. Your faith in me means more than words can express.

To the critics and early readers who provided honest feedback, thank you for helping shape this novel into its best form. Your insights were invaluable.

Finally, to every reader who picks up this book, you are the reason stories live and breathe. I hope this tale not only entertains but also provokes thought about the paths we choose and the forces that shape us.

Let the journey begin…

Content

Smokey Sky

Zunaid stood by the window and his small hands gripped the metal bars as he looked longingly at his parents walking down the street. His face was still streaked with the remnants of dried tears. He had cried and pleaded for over an hour to accompany them to the market. But his persistent habit of throwing tantrums for toys, sweets, and anything flashy had made his parents sternly refuse his demand.

The seven-year-old kid left behind felt like a punishment far more painful than it was meant to be. His parents were familiar with his tendency to sneak out and hide at neighbours' homes and thus, had no choice but to lock the front door from the outside. It wasn't an uncommon practice in their home since Zunaid's impulsive nature had led to such precautions being taken often.

From the window, he yelled out for his mother, hoping that her heart would melt and she would turn around. But his cries were worthless and he could hear the fading sound of footsteps. Eventually, the silence became too loud to bear. He left the window and wandered up to the terrace. This small, cluttered space felt more like his private territory where he usually spent time when he was sad or crying.

Tucked under a broken wooden shelf, there was a large jar filled with his treasured collection of marbles. He pulled it out with care, sat cross-legged on the warm cement floor and began counting them one by one. He recounted them three times before letting out a deep, frustrated sigh and heading back down to the kitchen, hoping to distract himself with food.

The kitchen was modest in size, just eight feet by five feet. Along one wall was a working shelf cluttered with a gas stove, a pressure cooker, a few steel utensils, and some scattered spices. At the far end of the shelf was a sink, slightly rusted at the corners. Above the shelf were wooden cabinets installed about six feet high, filled with jars of homemade snacks and dry foods. Zunaid knew that one of these jars had something special, biscuits and chips that were reserved only for visiting guests. His mother was particular about not letting him touch it, which, of course, made it all the more tempting.

He walked into the drawing room and fetched a lightweight plastic stool. Though wobbly and visibly cracked at the base, it was the only option for Zunaid to reach the compartment. He dragged it across the kitchen floor, ignoring the cracks. With cautious determination, he positioned the stool directly under the cabinet and began climbing. The stool quivered beneath his weight, and fear crept into his chest. He grabbed the cabinet handle with one hand to get some stability and reached for the jar with the other.

His fingers barely grasped the edge of the jar when he let go of the cabinet door to hold the jar properly. That single movement was enough. The stool slipped and the jar slid from his hands, and before he could regain his balance, Zunaid crashed to the cement floor with a loud thud. The jar shattered beside him. The world went black.

A thunderous boom ripped through the air, a sound so sharp and deep it was as if the earth had cracked open. The windows rattled violently. Birds scattered from rooftops in frantic flocks. The noise echoed for nearly a kilometre, leaving the neighbourhood in stunned silence. For a few seconds, everything stood still.

People emerged from their homes, frozen with confusion. Mothers held their children tightly, eyes wide with fear. Men and young boys ran out into the street, scanning the horizon for smoke or flame. The noise hadn't come from Zunaid's house, it came from the direction of the main market street, some metres away.

Zunaid lay unconscious in the kitchen, his small body crumpled beside the broken pieces of plastic and blood dripping from his elbow and one calf. He was unaware of the sirens that began to wail in the distance, or the rush of feet echoing through the neighbourhood lanes.

The main market in the old quarter of Srinagar had always been a busy place packed with locals to get their daily essentials. Rows of shops flanked both sides of the street, selling everything from groceries to mobile phones, from clothes to Kashmiri handicrafts. Tea stalls lined the corners where men in pherans would gather, sipping kehwa and sharing stories of politics and weather. On weekends, the market thrived with even more vigour, vendors with carts of fruits and roasted nuts, people almost pushing each other to move from one place to another and children running past shops.

And among that chaos, a parked scooter had become the vehicle of destruction.

The scooter had stood there for several hours, covered in dust and age. It hadn't raised suspicion as old two-wheelers were common in the area. But unknown to the vendors and customers nearby, it had been rigged with a powerful explosive, an improvised explosive device (IED) planted with strategic intent, and it detonated leaving a brutal impact.

The blast radius extended around fifty meters, shredding the surrounding area. People closest to the explosion, those standing beside the scooter, shopkeepers by the entrance, passersby, were instantly killed. The force of the explosion was so huge that the temporary stalls adjacent to the place of incident were completely demolished and debris was flying across the street. Glass windows shattered in a wave of sharp rain, while several walls cracked. The flames that followed the blast engulfed clothes hanging on balconies of some houses.

Bodies were scattered across the street, some lifeless, while others writhing in pain. Blood stains coloured the entire pavement, mixing with dust and rubble. People were screaming, the wounded cried for help. The air was filled with the harsh, and unpleasant smell of smoke, blood, and burning plastics and clothes.

The local police arrived within minutes, their sirens cutting through the thick air. Officers jumped out of their vehicles, weapons raised, scanning for additional threats. They pushed the crowd back, trying to secure the area and prevent further injuries.

Soon after, the army jeeps arrived and army officers dressed in their camouflage military green uniform, jumped out of their vehicles. Soldiers spread out swiftly, cordoning off the blast site.

They worked in coordination with bomb disposal units to ensure there were no secondary explosives hidden nearby.

Ambulances poured in with red and blue lights swirling over the carnage. Medics moved quickly, checking pulses, applying tourniquets, loading the injured onto stretchers. The dead were laid out on one side, covered with shrouds, sheets, tarps or anything available.

Soon media vehicles arrived on the spot. They were restricted from entering the incident spots. Live reporting started on local and national news channels. Reporters stood in front of the cordoned market, speaking solemnly into microphones, their voices barely audible over the noise of sirens and shouting. Within an hour, national news picked up the footage. It was broadcast across the country with images of smoke, shattered shops, people carrying the wounded, bodies lying motionless on bloodied streets.

"Breaking News: Blast in Srinagar Market—At least 20 Dead, Dozens Injured."

"Suspected Terror Attack in Srinagar."

"India under Attack: Kashmir on Target."

The images spread like wildfire on social media. Debates and politicians' speeches started on news channels with reasons, probable people or terrorist organisations involved, their perspectives and the needed actions. Defence ministry was being questioned on the lack of intelligence information and failure of preventive measures. A sense of fear rushed along the citizens of the country.

The police started examining the disaster zone. Forensic team reached and started collecting samples. The scooter's charred frame was roped off, carefully photographed, and analysed for evidence. Burned documents, scorched ID cards, even melted pieces of mobile phones were collected and tagged.

Shopkeepers stood nearby in disbelief, some sobbing, others staring at the charred remains of their stores as many of them had lost their livelihood in minutes.

While everything was falling apart in the city, Zunaid lay unconscious in his kitchen, bleeding slowly, the pool of blood growing around him. The bleeding was getting dangerously serious and time was running out. But Zunaid was alone.

One of the neighbours, Hameed, had heard about the blast in the market and was growing anxious. He knew Zunaid's parents had left for some place, but was not sure where. That made him uneasy. He was also aware that they generally locked Zunaid home while going to some local places.

He walked to Zunaid's main door and knocked. "Zunaid?" he called out. There was no reply. He knocked harder and shouted louder, "Zunaid! Can you hear me?"

Still, there was no sound or any movement from inside.

Worried something terrible might have happened, Hameed looked around. He picked up a stone lying near the roadside and started hitting it hard against the door's lock. Again and again, the stone clanged against metal until the lock finally broke loose with a loud snap. The door creaked open, and he rushed inside, calling Zunaid's name.

As soon as he stepped into the hall, he got a glimpse of a head just barely visible at the entrance of the kitchen. His heart dropped. He sprinted forward and saw the boy lying on the cold floor, unconscious, blood spread across the tiles like someone had spilled red paint.

"Zunaid!" he cried and knelt beside him. Without wasting a second, he lifted the boy gently in his arms and ran outside, screaming, "Someone bring a vehicle! We need to take him to the hospital fast!"

Neighbours ran out of their homes, shocked, scared, while someone quickly brought out a scooter. Hameed got on, holding Zunaid tight, and rushed to the nearest hospital.

But what he saw there was something he could never have imagined.

The hospital was flooded with people, men, women, children, some crying, some bleeding, some collapsed on the floor. There were injured people everywhere, lying on the corridors, on stairs, even outside the hospital gate. People were screaming. Doctors and nurses were running from one ward to another, trying their best, but the sheer number of patients was overwhelming.

There was no stretcher available for Zunaid. No wheelchair either. So, they laid him on a white bedsheet someone had spread on the floor of the general ward. Blood was being wiped from the floor every few minutes, only for more to flow again.

A nurse hurried over, gave Zunaid a couple of injections and dressed his wound. Then they waited, hoping he would regain consciousness.

After some time, Zunaid slowly opened his eyes and looking around to get totally confused. His lips were dry. He blinked, trying to understand where he was, but he couldn't make sense of anything.

Hameed leaned in and softly asked, "Zunaid... where are your parents? Do you know where they went?"

The boy whispered, barely able to speak, "Market."

Hearing this, Hameed's face went pale. His heartbeat quickened. He knew what had happened in the market. A chill ran down his spine as he imagined the worst.

He immediately took Zunaid back home. On the way, he tried to stay calm, tried not to panic, but he was shaking inside. His mind was racing.

Back at home, he handed Zunaid over to his wife, asking her to keep him keep warm and give him some water. Then he rushed out again, this time heading straight to the market to the disaster zone.

What he saw there was worse than any nightmare. The entire place was in ruins. Shops were half-burnt, glass pieces scattered everywhere. Shoes, bags and broken goods lay across the street. Police and army officials were keeping people away. Ambulances were coming and going, sirens wailing non-stop.

Hameed searched every corner, looked under the broken stalls and asked every official he saw. Then a constable agreed to help him. "We are identifying the dead. You can check," he said.

Hameed followed him quietly as the constable walked to a side area where bodies were lined up and covered with pieces of clothes. The constable started removing the cloth from the faces of the bodies one by one, and with each face he saw, he found relief that it was not from the faces he was looking for.

"No, not her, not him," Hameed continued as he tried scanning every face.

Some faces were burnt. Some bodies weren't complete, people too close to the blast had their body parts scattered, and the police had already cleared a few such bodies from the spot.

After an hour, Hameed still hadn't found them. But he couldn't give up yet. He ran to the hospital again, this time hoping to find them among the injured. He checked every ward, every corridor, and ran in all corners for help.

Finally, one nurse nodded. "Come with me," she said, leading him to a ward where the most critical patients were kept.

On a small bed in the corner, lay a woman with her face bandaged and arm wrapped thickly with cotton and plaster. Her right limb was missing from the knee down. Her face had deep cuts, and she looked unconscious.

It was Zunaid's mother. Hameed stepped closer and froze. He couldn't believe the state she was in. His eyes filled with tears, but he wiped them quickly. He had to be strong.

He asked the nurse about her condition, but she had no time to talk. "So many patients, sir… we're doing everything we can," she said and rushed off.

Hameed looked among other faces lying there to find Zunaid's father, but didn't succeed. He spent the rest of the evening searching for him, checking hospitals, asking around, but there was no sign.

Finally, he was left with no other option and made his way back home. As he walked into his colony, he felt like he had entered a battlefield. Bodies lay outside homes, some covered in bedsheets, some being bathed in preparation for burial. People were crying, loudly, painfully, wailing in the streets. A few injured people sat beside their dead family members, weeping silently. Hameed had never seen this much pain, this much death in one place.

He walked into his house, shoulders drooped. Zunaid was sitting up on the bed, looking a little better with a blanket wrapped around him. His eyes were tired but searching.

As soon as he saw Hameed, he asked, "Uncle… Ammi and Abbu haven't come back yet. Do you know where they are?"

Hameed had no answer. He opened his mouth but couldn't speak. What could he say? That his mother might not survive? That his father hadn't even been found?

He turned away, tears silently rolling down his face. His wife understood something was not right. They both walked out of the room and Hammed told everything to his wife. She couldn't understand how to react. She managed to gather herself and went back inside and told Zunaid, "They might have gone to your uncle's place. They should return by tomorrow."

Zunaid felt sad, innocently thinking why he wasn't taken along, unaware of the incident that had happened.

That night only the children slept, while no one else in the colony could close their eyes. Grief had swallowed the whole place. Some were preparing for the funerals of their loved ones. Others were still searching for answers, for names, for people who hadn't come home.

Hameed, along with a few other men from the colony, spent the night looking for Zunaid's father and a few others who were still missing. As the hours passed, hope faded like the night sky before dawn.

Late into the night, Hameed went back to the hospital. He had been checking on Zunaid's mother, who had been fighting for her life. But when he arrived, the nurse at the desk shook her head softly. Zunaid's mother had given up fighting the battle to survive. The weight of sorrow was growing heavier by the minute.

As he prepared to take her body home for the final rites, Hameed noticed a large crowd near the hospital reception. A list had been pinned on a notice board with the names of those who had already been buried by the authorities, since their bodies were so badly damaged that they couldn't be handed back to families.

He moved closer, dread pressing against his chest and scanned the list to find Zunaid's father's name. His search was finally over.

With a heavy heart, he returned to the colony at dawn, bringing with him the body of Zunaid's mother and others from the community. The sun was just beginning to rise, casting a dull light over the grief-stricken homes.

Now, it was time to tell Zunaid the truth.

The boy had been resting under the effect of strong painkillers. His body was injured, but his soul was about to break in ways no medicine could help.

Hameed's wife stepped into the room quietly and sat beside him. She gently placed her hand on his forehead and said, in a soft, trembling voice, "Beta... your Abbu and Ammi are not coming back."

Zunaid blinked, his sleepy eyes still clouded. "Not coming back today also?" he asked, confused, expecting them to walk in any minute.

Outside the room, Hameed was listening. He couldn't stay silent. His voice cracked as he stepped in and said, "They're not coming back... ever. They both died in the bomb blast yesterday."

Zunaid stared at them, frozen. No tears, no sound. Just silence.

He sat up slowly, still not fully understanding. His lips parted slightly, as if to say something, but no words came. His eyes were wide, looking around the room, searching for his parents.

Then, he lowered his head, resting it on his knees. He didn't cry. It was as if his young heart had locked itself away, too shocked to feel anything.

That morning, the colony gathered for the burials. The bodies were wrapped in white shrouds, simple and still. Men stood in lines, offering prayers with soft voices and trembling hands. The women stood at a distance, some holding each other, others staring into the ground.

Zunaid was there, too, sitting quietly beside Hameed. His face was blank, pale. He didn't move much, didn't speak. When his mother's body was lowered into the ground, he just stared at the cloth that covered her face.

As soil was gently poured over the graves, the sound of it falling was the only thing that seemed real to him. The prayers ended. People started walking back, some with slow steps, others wiping their eyes. But Zunaid didn't move. He stayed beside the grave until Hameed finally lifted him up in his arms. The boy leaned his head on Hameed's shoulder, silent still, his eyes wide open lost in a world that had changed forever.

A month had passed after the incident. The debates over terrorism reduced, the topics of news channels changed to new incidents from across the country, and people slowly forgot something happened in Srinagar. But the people of Srinagar did not forget, especially those who suffered losses of life.

The government offered money to those who had lost their homes or family members, hoping it would help them rebuild their lives. But money couldn't fill the silence left behind. The market started becoming busy again people slowly tried going back to their normal life routine.

Zunaid had changed. The cheerful and mischievous boy was gone. After the tragedy, he went to live with his uncle Imran, who lived just a few kilometres away from his old home. At school, he stayed quiet. The teachers understood his pain and didn't push him to speak or participate. He no longer played with his friends. He didn't ask for toys or treats anymore. The things that once made him happy didn't matter now.

His uncle hoped time would heal him and decided not to force anything. He believed that one day, Zunaid would return to his old self.

One day, as Zunaid walked home from school, a boy around 20 years of age approached him. His name was Saif. He looked at Zunaid and said gently, "You lost your parents in the blast. I did too. We're going through the same pain."

Zunaid stopped. It was the first time in weeks he felt something. He felt a connection of pain.

"You also lost both your parents?" Zunaid asked softly.

"Yes," Saif replied. "My Abbu and Ammi had gone to buy clothes for my birthday. But they never came back."

As he said this, tears rolled down his cheeks. Without another word, he turned and walked away.

Zunaid stood silent and didn't know what to say or do. He was too young to comfort someone else, but could understand that pain as it was his own too. That night, he couldn't stop thinking about the boy.

A few days later, he saw him again.

"Do you miss your parents?" Saif asked. "Why did this happen to us? What did we do wrong?"

Zunaid didn't have the answers. But before he could say anything, the boy pulled out a small piece of sweet from his pocket.

"My parents used to bring this for me," he said. "Now, I don't like eating it alone. Do you want to share?"

Zunaid nodded and took the piece. That small gesture meant more than words. From that day on, they started meeting often. Zunaid only opened up to him.

Saif became Zunaid's only friend, the only one who truly understood what he was feeling. They would talk for a while, often remembering their parents, sometimes crying silently together.

One day, Saif asked, "Do you ever wonder who did this?"

Zunaid looked down and whispered, "I don't know. But whoever did it… he will never be forgiven."

For the next few days, Saif brought up the questions again and again. "Zunaid, I know our parents can't come back. But what if this happens again? What if more kids lose their families? Don't you think we should find out who did this?"

Zunaid looked at him, curious. "But how? That's the job of the police."

Saif shook his head. "The police won't do anything. If they wanted to, they would have found out by now."

Zunaid stayed quiet, but something inside him agreed. It had been so long, and still there were no answers.

Then Saif said, "My uncle knows some important people. I'll ask him to find out who was behind the blast."

Zunaid's eyes lit up. "Really? And then what?"

"First, we find out who did it. Then we'll see what we can do to stop them from hurting anyone else."

Zunaid thought about it for a moment and finally said, "Please ask your uncle soon. I don't want anyone else to go through what we are going through."

They stood there for a few more seconds before parting ways again.

Zunaid walked home, feeling something he hadn't felt in a long time. He had hope for a better tomorrow at least for others.

Saif did not meet Zunaid for a few weeks and each passing day made Zunaid more and more anxious. He missed his friend, but more than that, he was worried. What if something bad had happened? What if Saif had faced the same fate as their parents?

One afternoon, while returning from school, Zunaid spotted a familiar figure at a distance. His eyes widened when he saw it was Saif. Without wasting a second, Zunaid ran as fast as he could towards him.

"Where were you?" he asked, panting. "Where have you been all these days? Are you alright?"

Saif looked at him and saw the concern in his eyes. He gave a faint smile and replied, "I went to meet my uncle. He lives far from here, and it took me some time to come back."

Zunaid was curious. "Did he find out anything about the blast?"

Saif looked around, as if checking to see if anyone was listening. Then he leaned closer and whispered, "I need to tell you something important."

Zunaid's eyes grew wide. He nodded, waiting for Saif to answer.

Saif continued, "My uncle said he can't tell everything directly. But he has a plan. He's getting people like us ready. People who have lost their parents in the blasts. He said we need to make sure it never happens again. He asked me to join them."

Zunaid was confused. "What kind of group is this? Where will we have to go?

"They are people like us," Saif replied. "And there's a place a bit far from here. If you want, you can come with me. I'm leaving tomorrow. But you must keep it a secret. Don't tell anyone. If my uncle finds out, he'll get angry at me."

Zunaid left the place with a big confusion. He wanted to know who killed his parents and join those people having the same pain. But he wasn't sure how he could leave his uncle and go to an unknown place. It was a dilemma for the eight-year-old kid.

That night, he lay on his bed staring at the ceiling. His thoughts kept spinning. The silence of the night did not help. He kept thinking about what Saif had told him. Finally, tiredness took over, and he fell asleep.

The next morning, Zunaid quietly took the photo of his parents from the wall, tucked it carefully in his bag, and left the house. He was supposed to go to school, but he didn't. Instead, he went to the spot where he usually met Saif. He waited there for hours, but Saif didn't show up.

That's when he realized that Saif might only come at the usual time after school. But it was too late to go back now. He didn't want anyone to know what he was doing. So he sat in a garden nearby, waiting.

Time passed slowly. Another hour went by. Then finally, he saw Saif walking towards the garden. He jumped up and ran to him.

"I am leaving today," Saif said.

"I want to come with you," Zunaid replied, his voice filled with determination.

Saif looked at him. A brief, almost hidden smile crossed his face. But he quickly changed his expression and asked, "Are you sure?"

Zunaid nodded. "Yes. I want to meet your uncle."

"Alright," Saif said. "Follow me. Tonight, we will stay at a friend's house. Tomorrow early morning, we'll leave."

As they walked, Zunaid asked, "Do you know the way? Who will take us there?"

"My uncle has sent someone to guide us," Saif said. "There are others like us too. They will be coming with us."

By evening, they reached the outer part of Srinagar. It was a quiet, isolated area. A jeep was waiting outside a small house. Nearby, Zunaid noticed a man standing with two other boys, one about his age, and the other, a teenager.

As they approached the jeep, Saif reminded Zunaid, "Don't ask too many questions. We don't know them, and they may not like being asked."

Zunaid nodded silently.

They all got in the jeep and the person waiting for them jumped in the driver's seat and drove them. It was a two-hour drive on the curvy Himalayan terrain and the vehicle stopped next to an open field. It was in the Kupwara region and they were close to the LOC (Line of Control) border of India and POK (Pakistan Occupied Kashmir). It was already dark and Zunaid wasn't feeling safe. But he had Saif along with him to give him confidence.

They walked across the field for a kilometre. In the distance, they saw a small hut with light coming from inside. As they stepped in, they saw a kind-looking lady who had prepared dinner for them. The smell of food made Zunaid's stomach growl. He hadn't eaten since morning.

The group sat down in a queue on the floor. The lady served them hot mutton curry, rice, and rotis. Zunaid ate heartily, feeling both comforted and exhausted.

After the meal, the man who had driven the jeep spoke, "Rest for a while. We'll leave soon."

Zunaid was puzzled and whispered to Saif, "Where are we going now? You said we will leave tomorrow morning."

Saif leaned in and whispered back, "Just a few more kilometres and we will reach. I told you that the place is a bit far. But don't worry. Once we reach you can have a good sleep."

Zunaid trusted him, so he stayed quiet. Everyone lay down for a short rest. After some time, they all got up and started walking again. This time, the path led them through a dense jungle and over some low mountains. It was a long walk, and Zunaid was getting tired. But he kept going, following the group.

After nearly an hour, they reached a narrow stream. The person who had guided them till that point stopped there and asked others to cross to find another person waiting. The water was low, just some small stagnant pools scattered around.

They crossed it easily. On the other side, another man was waiting. He didn't speak much, just signalled them to follow him.

They walked for about thirty more minutes, and finally saw another jeep parked under the trees. The new man drove this one. They all got in again, and the journey continued in complete silence.

Zunaid, without even realizing, had left his country unofficially, unaware of the place and the situation he was heading to.

Resolution

Imran was growing more anxious with each passing hour. He searched all the nearby colonies, walking street after street, asking everyone he came across if they had seen Zunaid. There was no sign of him. With hope still flickering, he walked the long way to his school, checking the park on the route, hoping Zunaid might be there. But the park was empty, and so was the school. He looked everywhere he could think of. The afternoon sun dipped slowly, and the sky turned grey as evening crept in. The light faded, and worry turned to panic. Still, there was no trace of Zunaid.

With a heavy heart and trembling legs, Imran made his way to the police station. He approached the officer at the desk and explained everything. He gave Zunaid's name, age, school, appearance and all other details he could recall. The officer listened carefully and then asked, "Where are his parents?"

Imran swallowed hard and replied, "They died in the Srinagar market blast."

The officer's expression changed instantly. His face tensed, eyes narrowing slightly, as if he had connected some unseen dots. Imran noticed it and quickly asked, "What happened, Sir?"

The officer hesitated for a moment and then spoke in a serious tone. "There have been cases… cases where children who lost their families were brain-washed, misled and taken to terrorist training camps in the POK region."

Imran felt like the ground beneath him had disappeared. Terrorist camps? Zunaid? The thought itself was unbelievable. His little cousin, who still couldn't tie his shoelaces properly, how could anyone think he'd end up in a place like that?

Trying to stay calm, Imran gave more details like Zunaid's nature, his likes and fears and his behaviour in recent weeks. The officer noted everything and immediately passed on the information through his walkie-talkie. The alert was sent to all nearby police stations, especially the ones near the border. Even the army headquarters in Srinagar was informed. A wide search operation began at once.

Police jeeps and army vehicles started moving across the region, especially near the border areas where crossing was possible. They searched the forests, the narrow tracks, and even the smallest of paths that led towards the border. Night passed into morning, but no clue was found. The tension only grew.

The next day, as soon as the school reopened, police officers reached the school to ask the teachers and students if anyone had seen Zunaid or noticed anything unusual.

The investigation went on in probable areas from where border crossing was possible, and information was found of a kid spotted in uniform in the Kupwara region.

By evening, the horrifying news reached the police station. Based on gathered information and confirmation from sources, it was suspected that Zunaid had indeed crossed the border and was now in a terrorist training camp in POK.

Imran was crushed. He couldn't believe it. Tears welled up in his eyes as he walked back home, feeling emptier than ever. In his heart, he feared the worst. It felt like he had lost the last piece of his brother's family.

Across the border, a new life had begun for Zunaid. It was a life far different from anything he had known before. The camp spread across a vast stretch of land and was both quiet and intimidating. It covered several acres and had a mix of flat plains, hilly stretches, and patches of water bodies that glistened under the sun. This terrain, though not naturally beautiful, had been carefully chosen. It was remote and hidden, away from the eyes of the world. Surrounded by dense tree lines on some sides and rocky ridges on others, the place was difficult to access and even harder to escape from.

On the flat land stood the heart of the camp with rows of permanent buildings constructed with concrete and metal sheets. These were plain structures with no signs, no decorations, and no colours. They looked more like storage units or abandoned factories than living quarters. Some of these buildings were always guarded, with stern-looking men posted at the doors, their eyes sharp and unreadable. These particular buildings were strictly out of bounds for the trainees. Nobody questioned what went on inside them. Rumours floated around with some saying it was where weapons were stored, others believed they were used for planning operations or interrogations. The truth was never discussed aloud.

The other buildings on the flat ground were used as dormitories for the trainees. Long narrow halls, filled with mattresses lying on the ground, made up their living space. Each trainee had a thin mattress, a small wooden box for personal belongings, and a woollen blanket that barely fought off the cold during nights. There were no fans or heating systems. The windows were barred, and lights were turned off strictly at a fixed time every night.

Next to the dormitories stood the mess hall, a long, echoing building where meals were served twice a day. The food was basic and mostly flatbread, lentils, and sometimes rice. Meat was rare and only appeared on special days, often when someone completed a major task or when a leader visited the camp. The men stood in lines, ate in silence, and left as soon as they were done. Talking during meals was discouraged. The atmosphere was heavy with discipline.

Beside the mess was an old building that looked like it had been there long before the camp was built. Its walls were cracked and vines had begun to crawl up its sides. This was the classroom. Here, the trainees were taught the ideology behind their mission. Hours were spent in this room, listening to speeches and watching videos. The instructors spoke with fire in their voices. They used stories, history, and religion to justify their actions.

A little distance from the dorms and classroom, there was a huge open ground. It stretched far and wide, an uneven piece of land with patches of dry grass, some gravel, and a few trees at the edges. This was the training field. Every morning, before sunrise, the trainees gathered here for physical training. Under the sharp whistles of their instructors, they ran laps, climbed ropes, crawled through mud, jumped over walls, and practiced endurance. The mornings were cold, but sweat poured down their faces as they pushed their bodies to the limit.

In one corner of the ground, there was a shooting range. Wooden dummies and metal targets were lined up against mounds of dirt. The sound of gunfire echoed through the camp daily. Instructors taught them how to hold, aim, and fire different kinds of weapons. From pistols to assault rifles, from grenades to rocket launchers, each weapon had its own place in their daily routine.

Beyond the training field, the land rose into a series of small hills. Some of these were used for tactical exercises. The trainees practiced ambush techniques, stealth movement, and simulated attacks. Smoke bombs were used during drills, and the air would often smell of burnt chemicals. The instructors were harsh, shouting, punishing, correcting their moves and even abusing at times. Discipline was everything there. One wrong step could earn a trainee an hour of extra physical punishment or a day without food.

Near the hilly terrain, a shallow stream ran through the edge of the camp. The stream, though not very deep, served as a water source and sometimes as part of their survival training. Trainees were taught how to hide in water, cross rivers silently, and use natural surroundings to their advantage.

There was a medical tent run by a stern man with little patience. He treated injuries quickly and without sympathy. Bandages, antiseptics, and a few basic medicines were all they had. Serious injuries meant being sent away, sometimes never to return.

Scattered across the camp were small lookout posts, wooden towers or elevated platforms where guards kept watch day and night. The camp was under constant surveillance. Cameras were fixed at certain points, and drones were sometimes flown for external monitoring. The trainees were always aware that they were being watched, even when they were alone.

Right from the very first day, Zunaid was made to believe that he had a mission—a mission that was personal and painful. The trainers didn't waste any time. They told him and the other new recruits that they weren't there by chance. They were there for a reason, and that reason was revenge. It was not just any revenge but the revenge of their parents, their relatives, and everyone they had lost. The pain of those deaths was turned into a weapon. And slowly, that weapon was placed in their hands.

They were told that their loved ones had been killed by the Indian Army. Not just soldiers, but Indian citizens too. "They don't want Muslims in their country," the trainer said again and again. "They hate you. They hated your father, your mother, your people. And they still hate you. That's why they killed them. And they're still killing more, every single day."

Zunaid had never seen the enemy with his own eyes, but the stories were enough. Day after day, night after night, the same words were repeated. They showed them fake, edited videos but no one questioned it. They played recordings of women crying, of children screaming, of explosions in villages. Each sound made Zunaid's heart feel heavy. And with that heaviness came anger. The kind of anger that doesn't go away. The kind that needs someone to blame.

He was young and hurt. And they knew it. That's what they wanted. Young boys like Zunaid who were full of emotion, who had lost someone, who didn't know the full truth. They used that pain like fuel. They turned it into hate. And the more Zunaid listened, the more he started to believe everything. He began to see the world differently. Everything was now black and white. India was the enemy. Its people were the enemy. They were the reason for his suffering.

He didn't know how or when it happened, but slowly his thoughts were no longer his own. The words of his trainers echoed in his mind even when they weren't around. They had planted a seed of revenge and it was growing fast. He felt proud when they called him a fighter. He felt strong when they told him he was chosen for something big., something meaningful. And even though he had never held a gun before, he was now being trained to kill.

The brainwashing was just the beginning. Once Zunaid and the others were fully convinced of their purpose, the real training began. It wasn't just about learning to fight but turning them into weapons. Weapons that didn't question orders. Weapons that followed hate without hesitation.

Every day started early. Before the sun could rise, they were already lined up outside. The cold wind didn't matter. The hunger didn't matter. The only thing that mattered was discipline. They were trained to forget pain, to forget comfort. The trainers shouted, hit, punished, whatever it took to break their softness. "Weakness is death," they said. "Only the strong can bring justice."

Zunaid was not used to such a life. At first, he struggled. The heavy running, crawling through mud, climbing walls, carrying weights, it all pushed his body to the edge. His muscles ached, his feet bled, and his breath always felt short. But he never said a word. The stories they had told him about his parents, about his people, they echoed louder than his pain. So, he pushed on. He wanted revenge more than he wanted rest.

Soon, they moved to weapons training. Rifles, pistols, grenades, they were all laid out in front of him like toys for a child. The first time Zunaid held a gun, his hands shook. But his trainer placed a hand on his shoulder and said, "This is the tool of freedom. Use it wisely. Use it for your people."

They taught him how to aim, how to shoot without blinking, how to reload without thinking. It wasn't just about pulling the trigger. It was about doing it with purpose. They showed him how to stay low, how to move without making noise, how to vanish into shadows. Every move had a reason. Mistakes were punished, sometimes harshly. But that was the point. They were not building soldiers, they were building machines.

Zunaid was also taught how to build and plant explosives. How to time them, how to escape before they blew up. It was dangerous, but no one cared. They made it sound noble. "A single blast," the trainer said, "can shake a whole city. Can send fear to the hearts of millions. That is power. That is justice."

There were also lessons in survival. How to hide in forests. How to stay alive without being seen. They said, "You might be alone out there. You might be behind enemy lines. But remember, the mission is bigger than you. Even if you die, you will die a hero."

The most difficult part was not the physical pain. It was mental training. They were taught to hate without doubt, taught to follow orders without asking questions, taught to see Indians as threats, even children. "A child today can become a soldier tomorrow," the trainers said. "Don't feel sorry. Feel proud. You are doing this for your people."

Years passed and Zunaid became Omar, a trained terrorist who had already killed several people on both sides of the border by the age of seventeen. Crossing the LOC was a child play for him. He had encountered the Indian Army on certain occasions, but managed to escape safely each time taking the guard of villagers in the region. He became one of the best trained and most lethal terrorists of the group.

Once he was asked to move to Baramulla. The chill of early spring lingered in the air as Omar and his two companions made their way into the Baramulla region of Kashmir. Snow still clung to the edges of the pine-covered slopes, and a thick silence hung over the hills. He wasn't new to the place and had visited the region several times after his training, disguised as a local from that area, seeking information about police and army movements.

This time he arrived at the place for a specific task. One of the villagers in Baramulla had begun working with the Indian Army, giving up safe house locations and movement patterns. Two of their couriers had vanished without trace. Weapons that were supposed to be delivered had been intercepted. Omar had suspected a leak and his handlers had confirmed it. His task was to identify the person who had betrayed and eliminate him.

Omar's group had taken refuge in a burnt-out sheep shed on the edge of a village named Kansipora. His companions, Farooq and Bilal, waited silently as he surveyed the area. Through a crack in the wooden slats, Omar watched children playing near the edge of the stream, older women carrying bundles of firewood, and men sitting on low walls, talking in hushed voices. It was a peaceful place, but peace was always deceiving there.

That night, they met their contact, an old shepherd named Bashir, sympathetic to their cause. Over a weak fire and a tin pot of tea, Bashir confirmed what Omar had feared.

"There is one man," Bashir said, lowering his voice. "Rafiq, a tailor. His shop is in the market. Always listening, always asking questions. He has new friends in the army post. He goes at night. Quietly."

"How sure are you?" Omar asked.

"I've seen him. But more than that, since he returned from Srinagar last month, things have changed. He's not the same."

The next morning, as the sun filtered through the misty pine trees, Omar took slow sips of his tea, eyes fixed on the tailor shop across the street. Rafiq moved with calm, deliberate gestures, folding cloth, stitching, laughing with customers. But there was something unnatural about his ease. Too careful, too smooth. And more than once, Omar noticed the tailor glancing at uniformed men passing by, men who would sometimes nod back with a familiarity that no ordinary villager should have.

By noon, Omar had seen enough.

He returned to the shed in Kansipora. Farooq and Bilal waited, checking their bullets and their AK47.

"It's him," Omar said. "Rafiq is the leak. Bashir was right."

"When do we move?" Farooq asked.

"Tonight. When he visits the post. We follow him. Quietly."

They spent the afternoon planning the route and exit. Omar insisted on moving without gunfire if possible. A clean elimination without any noise and trail.

But Kashmir rarely allowed things to go as planned.

Night fell, and the village curled into its usual hush. Crickets chirped and dogs barked in the distance. In the fading moonlight, Omar and his men melted into the shadows. Rafiq's shop had long closed, and Omar had seen him step out alone an hour earlier, heading toward the eastern ridge which led to the direction of the army post.

"He's going to them," Omar muttered.

They trailed him through thickets and narrow trails, their breath misting in the cold. About twenty minutes into the walk, Rafiq paused near a tree, looked around, then tapped a small metal pipe against the ground - once, twice, thrice. A coded signal.

Moments later, a soldier emerged from the trees. Omar froze. A quiet exchange followed. Rafique handed something to the soldier, possibly a USB and then the soldier disappeared.

"That's it," Omar whispered. "He's one of them now."

Bilal raised his weapon, but Omar held his hand.

"Not here. Too close to their post. We wait."

They moved like shadows, keeping distance, careful not to snap twigs or shift rocks. Rafiq walked ahead, unaware, humming to himself, the cold air puffing around his mouth.

As Rafiq reached a narrow bend in the forest path, surrounded by tall deodar trees, Omar raised his hand. The three of them paused behind a low ridge. Omar stepped out alone, silent and steady.

Rafiq turned at the sound of footsteps behind him. His eyes widened when he saw Omar.

"You?" he said, voice barely a whisper. "What are you doing—"

The bullet entered his chest before he could finish. It was quick, clean shot. Rafiq gasped, stumbled back a few steps, and dropped to the ground. He lay there, twitching once. Then still.

Omar lowered his pistol and exhaled. "It's done."

Just then, a harsh voice cracked through the trees.

"Stop! Don't move!"

A searchlight burst open from the ridge. Omar ducked.

"Run!" he shouted, just as the first shots rang out.

Farooq and Bilal split off into the darkness, diving into the underbrush. Bullets tore through the trees, slicing bark and stirring up the ground. Omar rolled behind a boulder with his heart hammering in his chest. One shot ricocheted off the stone just inches from his head.

He crawled backwards, careful and quick, then slipped down a slope that led toward the edge of the village. The firing behind him grew louder with increasing voices, soldiers shouting and orders being given.

He had to vanish before being ambushed. Through the trees, the village lights flickered in the distance. He made for them, limping slightly. His leg had grazed a rock during the fall. He pressed forward, teeth clenched, moving from shadow to shadow.

Meanwhile, Bilal was shot while he was trying to run towards the denser part of the forest and there was no sign of Farooq.

Near the edge of a narrow field, Omar stopped. A small figure stood just ahead, staring toward the trees, curious and afraid. Omar saw a boy, seven or eight years old. Standing alone.

Omar looked back. The army was getting closer.

He stepped forward, fast and silent, and grabbed the boy from behind, clamping a hand over his mouth.

"Don't scream," he whispered. "You'll be fine. Just stay quiet."

The boy trembled in his grip.

Voices approached. Flashlights flicked over the field.

"There! I see someone!"

A beam of light landed on Omar and the boy. He turned sharply, dragging the child in front of him, with his AK47 nozzle raised to the side of the boy's head.

"Stay back!" he shouted. "Stay back or he dies!"

Everything froze. The soldiers stopped. One of them raised his rifle. Omar adjusted his stance, using the child as cover.

"Put your weapon down!" a voice ordered.

"Put yours down," Omar snapped. "Or I will shoot."

The boy whimpered. Omar held him tighter, scanning the trees.

Two soldiers tried to flank him, moving low from the sides. He noticed.

"Don't try it!" he yelled. "I swear, I'll do it!"

But they kept coming, careful, thinking he was bluffing.

Omar didn't wait. He moved fast, raised his rifle and fired a burst.

One soldier fell flat. The second managed to shoot, but missed. Omar fired again. The second took a bullet on his right calf and stopped moving ahead. The other soldiers were sure that Omar was in panic and could kill anyone including the child to save himself. As they did not want any civilian, that to a young kid to lose his life, they hesitated to step ahead.

To prevent any further damage, the soldiers dropped their weapon as Omar ordered and moved back a couple of stepped assuring Omar that they would not harm him and in return asked Omar to release the boy.

Omar pushed the boy away with full force towards the soldiers, and sprinted into the darkness before anyone could pick their weapons and aim. The boy fell down with his head hitting the side of a rock. Blood poured like a red fountain coming out of his head and within minutes the poor kid died due to head injury and severe bleeding.

The soldiers picked their weapon and ran the same direction. Shots rang out behind Omar. Dirt kicked up near his feet. A bullet ripped through the sleeve of his coat and he was shot on his forehand.

He still kept running through fields, across shallow streams, past haystacks and sleeping cattle. The village fell behind. He climbed the slope toward the pine woods, lungs burning, feet soaked in cold mud.

The mountain trail toward the Line of Control was narrow and hidden. He had memorized every turn during past missions. He didn't stop. As soon as he was about to cross the border, he found Farooq limping towards the border. Hearing the footsteps of Omar, he started running and tried taking cover, thinking him to be an army soldier. But when he noticed it to be Omar, he came out. A bullet had hit a side of his thing, scratching a part of the muscle, which was preventing him from walking fast. By the time the sun rose over the distant ridges, both Omar and Farooq were already on the other side of the LOC. Both were wounded but alive when they reached the camp.

Historical Bridge

A couple of years had passed since the last time Omar had narrowly escaped death. Life in the camp had returned to its usual rhythm. Omar now spent most of his days training new recruits of young men with angry eyes and a burning desire for revenge. They looked up to him, listened carefully to his words, and followed his every instruction. To them, Omar was a hero.

One calm afternoon, while Omar was teaching hand-to-hand combat to a group of new recruits, a black SUV rolled into the dusty campground. The vehicle was unfamiliar, and that alone was enough to draw everyone's attention. A few moments later, Zafar stepped out.

Zafar Raza Abdulla was a high-profile terrorist known all over the globe, and the major reason was his involvement in several terrorist activities carried out under is supervision in different parts of the world.

The sight of Zafar stunned everyone. Omar froze in place, his eyes fixed on the man walking with slow, powerful steps toward the main building. Zafar was not someone who appeared in camps like those. In fact, he had not been to that particular location in nearly five years. He was a high-value figure, one of the masterminds behind several large-scale attacks across India, especially in Srinagar and on military establishments. His name alone sparked fear across borders. That was why he remained hidden deep inside Pakistan, far away from any zone where Indian forces could get to him.

Realizing the importance of the moment, Omar quickly made his way toward Zafar. He greeted him with respect, bowing his head slightly. Zafar gave him a short nod and continued walking toward the restricted part of the camp about which Omar had only heard about, never seen.

To his surprise, Omar was asked to follow. This was the first time he had ever been called inside the restricted building. Only the most trusted and high-ranking operatives were allowed in. Omar's heart pounded with a mix of excitement and curiosity. He felt as though a door had just opened for him, one that led into the heart of power.

The building looked simple from the outside. It was made of concrete, painted in dull grey, and surrounded by tall metal fencing topped with barbed wire. A guard stood at the door holding an AK47, who stepped aside the moment Zafar approached. As they entered, the door shut behind them with a loud metallic thud.

Inside, the air felt cooler, and the walls were lined with heavy soundproofing material. They passed through a short hallway before stepping into a massive hall.

The hall was almost the size of a small airplane hangar. On one end were rows of black metal chairs facing the wall, which was covered with large, detailed maps. The ceiling was high, with exposed beams and soft yellow lights hanging low. There were several doors on both sides of the hallway leading into different rooms. As Omar followed Zafar, he glanced through the glass windows of the open rooms.

One room was filled with stacks of AK47 rifles piled up on wooden racks, their metal glinting in the low light. Another had rows of grenades stored in thick wooden crates, each labeled and numbered. One room had small drones lined up on shelves, while another had satellite phones, radio sets, and encrypted laptops neatly arranged on tables. There were a few rooms whose doors were tightly locked with no labels or windows, just silence behind those thick metal doors. Omar could only guess what lay behind them.

He had never imagined the scale of resources hidden within that building. Ammunition, technology, explosives, it was all there, ready for war. For a moment, he felt a chill run down his spine. But then, excitement took over. He had made it. He was now trusted enough to walk those halls.

As they reached the far end of the hall, Omar saw three enormous maps hanging on the wall. The first, nearly 10 feet by 10 feet, showed the entire region of Jammu and Kashmir with minute details covering towns, army bases, checkpoints, roads, and even the terrain lines. The second map was of the entire Indian subcontinent. The third focused solely on northeastern states of India.

Three other men, all experienced operatives, stood behind Zafar, all of them serious-faced and dressed in military fatigues. Zafar noticed Omar looking around, observing every detail, and smiled faintly.

"Take a seat, Omar," Zafar said, pointing to one of the black chairs.

Omar obeyed and sat down, his eyes still scanning the maps.

Zafar began, "We have three months to execute our plan. And I believe Omar is ready."

Omar nodded firmly, "I'm ready for whatever you say. Just give me the order."

Zafar leaned forward, resting his hands on the table. "Your success in the previous operations did not go unnoticed. You've proven yourself. That's why this time, we've chosen you for something very big."

He pointed to the map of India, specifically the northeastern region.

"It's time to take revenge for East Pakistan," he said coldly. "The way India took that land from us, this time, we'll take something from them. All seven northeastern states. We will separate them from India."

The room went silent for a moment before the others broke into low cheers of agreement.

Zafar continued, "This operation will require precision and planning. Omar, you will lead it. From now on, you are in charge. You will go to India, stay there for two months, collect all the necessary information, and return. After that, you will prepare the final strike. The plan must be executed on December 16th, the very day we lost East Pakistan."

Omar listened carefully, not missing a single word. Every detail mattered.

Zafar took out a thick folder from his bag and placed it on the table. "This has everything you need for your journey, fake documents, names of contacts, routes and hideouts. You'll study it carefully."

Omar reached out and picked up the folder. It felt heavy in his hands, not just with papers, but with responsibility.

The room went quiet again as Zafar looked him in the eye and said firmly, "Once you reach India, go straight to Delhi. Afzal will be waiting for you there. He will explain everything about the mission and our plan. He'll stay with you for the next two months. Keep sharing all the information you gather with him. Through our network, he will pass it on to the headquarters."

Omar nodded and asked, "What about the ammunition?"

Zafar replied, "Afzal has his own contacts. He'll arrange it for you. Just remember one thing, do not engage with the northeast militants. Any mistake there can put the entire mission in danger. Stay low, stay sharp. Take a good cover and return safely after collecting the information."

Omar took note of every detail, then looked at Zafar and said, "Thank you for trusting me. I will make sure this mission is a big success. I'll get ready and leave tonight."

Zafar nodded and wished him luck and went back to his meeting with the other members. Omar left the building quietly.

By evening, Zafar left the camp. Meanwhile, Omar started preparing to leave. He checked his bag, packed his essentials, and reviewed the route again. As the sun began to set, he left the camp. A jeep was waiting for him at the camp gate. It dropped him at the usual point near the border, a spot they had used many times before.

He stepped out of the jeep with his duffle bag and walked quietly towards the stream that marked the border. When he reached it, he found the water wild and rushing. It was the post-monsoon season, and the flow was stronger than usual. But Omar was trained for this. It didn't scare him.

Just as he was about to step into the water, he noticed something unusual on the other side. His instincts kicked in and stopped him. Slowly, he opened his bag and pulled out the night vision binoculars. Holding his breath, he looked through them and froze.

There was a new army post set up on the other side of the stream.

That wasn't there before. The entire zone had been quiet earlier, but after the last incident in the region, the Indian Army had increased patrols and checkpoints. Omar realized this could risk the entire mission. He couldn't afford a direct crossing anymore.

Without wasting a second, he changed direction and started walking north, staying close to the stream. He walked for hours in the dark. Ten kilometres later, he finally found a safer spot where the stream was narrow and the forest covered both sides. He crossed swiftly and quietly. But it was already dawn by the time he made it across.

The area he was in was filled with army presence. If anyone saw him, it could all be over. He rushed into a thick forest nearby and searched for cover. After walking for a while, he found a natural cave hidden under a slope, partially covered with bushes and moss. He crawled in and sat still.

Inside the cave, it was damp and cold with a mix of wet earth and dead leaves in the air. Omar pressed his back against the wall and closed his eyes for a moment, but only a moment. He couldn't afford to sleep.

Time seemed to slow down. Each minute felt like an hour.

His stomach growled, but he ignored it. He hadn't eaten since the night before. His throat was dry, but he had no water left. Still, it wasn't hunger or thirst that kept him alert, it was fear. Every sound outside made him freeze.

At one point, he heard the rustling of leaves with soft, slow footsteps. He stopped breathing.

He reached for his weapon, his hand moving slowly and silently. He listened carefully. The footsteps came closer, then stopped. Omar didn't move an inch. He heard the clinking of a rifle. Sweat rolled down the side of his face. He stared at the entrance of the cave, waiting for a shadow to appear. He knew that if the army suspected someone had crossed the border, they'd search every inch of this forest.

Then, the sound of boots crunching the forest floor faded. Whoever it was had turned away. Maybe they hadn't seen the cave, or maybe they had.

Hours passed. The forest was alive with tiny noises, branches swaying, birds flying, an occasional rustle of some animal in the leaves. But Omar knew the difference between wild movement and human footsteps.

The sun started to go down. Shadows stretched longer. Omar's legs had gone numb from sitting in the same position. His back ached. He was tired, hungry and cold, but he stayed still.

The forest was quieter now. The birds had gone silent, and the air had turned colder. Omar checked his watch. He had spent nearly twelve hours in that cave.

When the sky turned deep orange, he finally decided to move. He stepped outside slowly and listened. Just as he was about to walk, he heard soft crunching again. Someone was approaching.

He crouched low and drew his weapon, ready but silent.

Two army men appeared from behind the trees, scanning the area with their torches. Omar didn't move. He was hidden well behind the rocks. One of them came dangerously close and pointed his torch towards the trees nearby. Then, after a short exchange, they turned around and walked away.

Slowly, he kept moving, making halts after each kilometre to check for the surroundings before moving further, to ensure he wasn't detected. He was also surprised by the number of check posts and army soldiers deployed in that area which was way more than the regular count.

He took the isolated forests or rocky trails where no one was expected and by next morning, he managed to reach Srinagar and met Bashir.

Bashir, who was generally informed about anyone's arrival from the camp, was surprised to see Omar without any information.

Seeing Omar, "Bashir asked, "Omar! How come you are here? And there was no information shared."

Omar responded, "Something urgent came up. I need to stay at your place for today and I will leave at night."

Bashir was a bit hesitant and Omar was surprised to see his reaction and asked, "What happened? What is the problem?"

Bashir replied, "The army deployment is in huge numbers and it is very dangerous for you to be in Srinagar. The patrolling team keeps coming every now and then. And if they have any doubt, they search the house without any warrant or notice. I will recommend you to leave for Jammu immediately."

Omar was extremely tired and had no energy to move forward since he hadn't slept for 2 nights and kept walking all the distance. But he was left with no choice. He did not want his cover to be blown. He asked Bashir to prepare for breakfast. After having it, he changed his attire and wore the local outfit to blend in the crowd easily. He hid his weapon and took the fake Indian citizenship identity he received from Zafar and left for Jammu by local state bus. On reaching Jammu, he took a hotel and waited there for a day. From there he boarded the general compartment of a train going to Delhi.

The next day, Omar arrived at New Delhi Railway Station. The air was filled with noise and movement. Porters rushed by with towering luggage, children cried, vendors shouted out chai and samosas, and train horns echoed through the wide platforms. Omar kept his head low, blending in with the crowd, his duffle bag slung over one shoulder. His eyes scanned the signs above the exits until he finally spotted a small PCO booth tucked in a corner near the station exit.

He stepped inside, picked up the scratched black receiver, and dialed a number from memory. The line clicked.

A voice answered. "Hello?"

"Afzal," Omar said softly, "I've reached Delhi. Where are you?"

"Near Red Fort," came the calm reply. "There's a small printing press, Lal Darwaza Press. Take an auto. Ask for the Red Fort market. The press is behind it."

"Okay," Omar said and hung up.

Outside, the streets buzzed with activity. He hailed an auto-rickshaw and gave the driver the location. The auto sputtered through the tangled lanes of Old Delhi, past spice shops and cycle repair stalls, fruit vendors yelling prices, and cows wandering freely on the road and carrying the scent of frying food, sweat and dust.

Twenty minutes later, the auto stopped in front of a nondescript shop. A faded signboard read: "Lal Darwaza Printing Press." The building was old, its walls cracked, paint flaking off like dry leaves. A musty smell of paper and ink hung around the place.

Omar stood outside, looking around. A few workers carried bundles of paper. Nobody paid him any attention. Ten minutes passed. Then, a man emerged from the alley beside the press.

He was around 40, about 5-feet 8-inches tall. Dressed in a white kurta-pyjama and a white kufi cap, his neatly dyed brown beard gave him a composed look. Soorma darkened his eyes, adding a strange sharpness to his gaze.

Afzal walked up, calm and purposeful. "You came on time," he said with a faint smile. "Come in."

They entered the press. Inside, machines hummed, ink rollers turned slowly, and the smell of paper was even stronger. Workers didn't glance at them, either too busy or too used to strangers.

Afzal pointed to a wooden bench. "Wait here. I'll be back."

He disappeared into a small room behind the machines. Omar sat, looking around. The place felt like a perfect cover, just another humble business in a busy market, hiding in plain sight.

After fifteen minutes, Afzal returned. "Let's go," he said.

They walked through the congested alleys of Old Delhi. The sun was harsh overhead. Two kilometres later, they reached a narrow lane filled with small houses lined side by side, one of the many chawls that dotted the area. Kids played with broken toys, women filled buckets from a public tap, and loudspeakers played old Bollywood songs from some neighbours' window.

"This way," Afzal said, leading Omar into a small, two-room house. The first room had a thin mattress, a ceiling fan that creaked, and a small cupboard. The second room was the kitchen, bare, except for a stove, a few steel plates, and a blue plastic drum of water. There was no attached toilet. The common washroom was fifty meters down the street, shared by the whole lane.

"This is home for now," Afzal said. "Quiet. Ordinary. Just the way we need it."

Omar sat on the mattress, wiping sweat from his forehead. "So, the plan?"

Afzal's expression turned serious. "No. Not here. Not even a word. Too many ears. Walls are thin. People are always around. One curious neighbour could ruin everything."

Omar nodded. "Understood."

Afzal poured him a glass of water. "You've got two days in Delhi. Finish what you came for. We leave after that."

That night, the heat lingered even after sunset. The fan barely helped. Omar lay awake, listening to dogs barking in the distance, rickshaws passing by, and the occasional murmur of voices from the lane. The mission was already in motion. He could feel it in his bones.

The next morning, Afzal left early for the press. He had built a strong fake identity as a man from Muzaffarpur in North Bihar working there to send money back home. Documents supported the story. People believed him as most of them were like him staying at that location, who came from different cities majorly from Uttar Pradesh and Bihar, to earn their living.

Omar, meanwhile, went to Jama Masjid, blending in with the crowd of worshippers. He moved with purpose, yet without drawing attention. By evening, both returned to the chawl.

Afzal asked casually, "Is the Delhi work done?"

Omar replied, "Yes. It's been initiated."

Afzal nodded. "Good. I've told at the press there's a medical emergency back home. I bought two tickets for Howrah. We leave tomorrow morning."

The next day, they boarded the train. As the train pulled out of New Delhi, a calm silence settled between them. It was a long journey, one and a half days of swaying coaches, chai vendors, and strangers making polite conversation. But they kept to themselves, speaking little, watching the countryside roll by.

By the time they reached Howrah, the sky was turning orange. The station was massive and chaotic. Omar stood still for a moment, looking at the huge arch of Howrah Bridge in the distance. The steel giant spanned across the Hooghly like a sleeping beast. He had seen pictures of it before. Now, it stood before him.

"Impressive," he said.

Afzal smiled. "Beautiful, isn't it? And fragile in the right place."

They walked across the bridge. The wind smelled of river and dust, people bustled on the sidewalks, and yellow taxis honked endlessly.

By the time they entered Kolkata city, it was night. They found a cheap lodge in a crowded area near Burrabazar. The room was small and hot, with peeling walls and a single fan. But it was enough.

"We need to talk," Omar said, after dropping his bag.

"Not here either," Afzal replied. "We'll eat first. Then I'll show you the place."

They went to a small dhaba nearby. Dal, rice, and fried fish filled their plates. Afzal barely spoke while eating. Omar knew he was thinking about the mission.

After dinner, they walked through the dim streets until they reached a dead-end railway line behind Kolkata station. It was late, close to midnight. The place was empty, quiet, and hidden from the city's eyes.

They sat on the cold tracks. Afzal finally spoke.

"Listen carefully. We will strike five times. Four initial blasts, followed by the real one."

"Where?" Omar asked.

"Howrah Bridge, Bodh Gaya, Deoghar Temple, and Kharagpur Station. All at once. Then, two hours later - Bagdogra Air Force Station."

Omar raised an eyebrow. "Bold."

"Strategic," Afzal said. "The first four will distract the nation. Panic will spread. Police and military will rush to those places. Bagdogra will be left exposed."

"And what happens after Bagdogra?"

"Our second team, trained separately, will cross into India from Nepal. Their goal will be to cut off the Northeast from the rest of the country. No supplies, no reinforcements. Total disruption."

Omar nodded slowly. "And we?"

"We ensure the first four blasts succeed. We scout each location, find security gaps, and monitor timings. We need to know everything, when guards change, when the crowd is thickest, and most importantly, where the weakest points are."

Omar leaned forward, his voice low. "How do we bring down the bridge?"

"There's always a weak spot," Afzal replied. "A structural joint, a stress point. One blast there and the whole thing will collapse. We'll study the bridge, every angle, every detail. We'll use cameras, visit as pedestrians, maybe even as maintenance workers."

"And the explosives have been arranged." Omar smiled faintly.

Afzal added, "For now, our job is surveillance."

They sat in silence for a while, watching a stray dogs cross the tracks in the distance.

Omar finally said, "You've thought this through."

Afzal looked at him. "We've waited too long for this. Every step must be perfect. We cannot fail."

They stood up and walked back to the lodge. The city slept on, unaware of the storm that was quietly forming in its shadow.

The next morning, they woke up early. The streets outside were already beginning to hum with life. Vendors were setting up their stalls, rickshaw-pullers stretched their limbs beside their vehicles, and the smell of tea brewing wafted in through the cracked window of their lodge room.

Omar and Afzal dressed up in plain clothes, cotton shirts, trousers, a camera hanging around Omar's neck, and a backpack slung over Afzal's shoulder. Their appearance was carefully chosen to blend in as ordinary tourists. Their movements needed to appear casual, their faces relaxed.

They left the lodge and made their way toward the famous Howrah Bridge. The sun had just started rising above the Hooghly River, casting golden reflections across the water. As they walked along the footpath of the massive steel bridge, the noise of honking taxis, impatient bus horns, and the constant hum of traffic surrounded them. The bridge shook slightly under the weight of the moving vehicles, but that was normal. That was how it always was.

They started observing every bolt, every joint, every beam carefully. They weren't there for sightseeing. They were studying the skeleton of the city's most iconic structure.

Omar pointed his camera towards the horizon but zoomed in instead on a set of riveted joints under one of the girders. "This section seems old," he said quietly.

Afzal nodded, eyes following the line of the steel. "We'll walk back and look at the joints on the eastern side next."

The two men crossed the bridge again, their pace slow, deliberate. They paused often, sometimes pretending to admire the view of the river, other times appearing to take pictures like any curious travellers. But their attention was locked on the structure itself. The bridge was a giant lattice of steel, complex and overwhelming. But they had done their research beforehand.

Howrah Bridge, also known as Rabindra Setu, was a cantilever bridge, built without any piers in the water. It rested entirely on two colossal pillars on either bank. Those pillars were deeply embedded in the earth and reinforced with heavy concrete and steel. They were nearly impossible to bring down, even with a large blast. That much, they knew already.

"Our focus should be on the joints and stress points," Afzal muttered, pausing near the middle span. "Not the pillars."

They examined the thick suspensions, the lower girders, and the steel trusses supporting the footpaths. Omar took discreet photographs from angles that seemed harmless. The angles, the shadows, the police patrol timing, all were being documented mentally.

Throughout the day, they walked across the bridge multiple times. Sometimes from the Howrah side, sometimes from the Kolkata side. They watched the flow of traffic, the heaviest load came during office hours in the morning and evening. They noted the spacing between the buses, the movement of taxis, and the occasional lorry loaded with goods. The vibration of the bridge changed with every heavy vehicle. The slight bounce, the way the steel responded, it all revealed secrets to trained eyes.

At around noon, they sat at a small tea stall near the bridge's Kolkata end. A group of college students was laughing over something nearby. The tea stall owner wiped glasses with a dirty rag and shouted orders to a helper.

Afzal stirred his tea slowly. "The best time will be during peak traffic," he said in a low voice. "More weight on the structure. More panic after."

Omar nodded. "We need to locate the nearest police presence as well. Reaction time will matter."

After finishing their tea, they resumed their work. This time, they roamed around the areas near both ends of the bridge. They searched for police outposts, observed patrol routines, and marked the positions of security cameras. There was a few traffic booths scattered around. They noticed a police jeep stationed on the Kolkata side, near the flower market entrance, and another at the Howrah end near the bus depot. Each location was mentally mapped.

They also visited the interiors of the bridge, walking underneath where possible, passing through small alleys and areas that tourists never ventured into. They noticed rust on some parts of the framework, areas where maintenance hadn't been carried out properly. Those were the spots they were interested in.

Later in the evening, they searched for historical maintenance records and structural evaluations of the bridge. Some of the reports were outdated, but still useful. They learned about the age of the structure which was over seventy years old and the constant stress it bore from the unending traffic.

"Even steel has a breaking point," Afzal whispered while scrolling through one report.

Omar didn't reply. His mind was busy calculating load pressures and blast radius based on the photographs and the angles they had studied. Numbers ran through his head quietly and clearly.

By the time it was sunset, the city was bathed in orange again. Streetlights began to flicker on. The river below turned darker, reflecting the shifting hues of the sky.

Afzal stopped near one of the supporting beams. He stared at it long and hard.

"This section," he said. "If we plant the device right here timed during morning rush, it will collapse one side enough to tear the structure."

Omar stared at it. He took one final photo. "We'll need exact measurements. I'll do that tomorrow."

By the time they returned to their lodge, it was dark. Their shirts were damp with sweat, and their legs ached from walking the entire day. Afzal dropped his bag to the floor and said quietly, "We've seen enough for today."

Omar nodded. He removed the camera's memory card and slipped it into a small envelope, placing it under the floorboard near the bed. "We'll review everything tonight."

For the next 3 days, they continued their observations on and around the bridge and collected sufficient information. They had every detail of the bridge, the traffic, the police, their response time and the overall damage they could cause.

In the night before leaving Howrah, Afzal organized all the details and stored them in a pen-drive.

Home of Gods

The next morning, the soft rays of the sun filtered through the dusty windowpane of their modest lodge room in Kolkata. The air was thick with humidity, and the honking of rickshaws had already begun outside. Omar and Afzal rose early, wasting no time. Their work at Howrah Bridge had been largely productive. It was time to move forward.

Their next destination was Deoghar, Jharkhand.

By late evening, they reached Jasidih Junction by train and from there took a shared auto-rickshaw to Deoghar town, a small but significant pilgrimage site in eastern India. The narrow lanes, lined with temples, dhabas, and shops selling flowers and religious items, were brimming with pilgrims dressed in saffron and white. The atmosphere felt sacred, almost untouched by time. The sound of bells echoed through the streets, and every second shop blared devotional songs through rusted speakers.

They checked into a small dharmshala posing as devotees who had come to seek blessings at the Baba Baidyanath Temple, one of the twelve Jyotirlingas and among the most revered Hindu shrines. The white structure with red borders rose majestically in the heart of the town. The temple complex was guarded, but not in a way that suggested constant vigilance. It was built for faith, not for fear.

That night, over a simple dinner of dal and rice in a crowded eatery, Afzal spoke in a low voice. "This temple is not just a spiritual centre, it is a symbol of faith. If it falls, the shock will echo through the country."

Omar nodded. "We'll have to be careful. The devotees here are alert, but the security is ritualistic. They don't expect an attack."

The next morning, they entered the temple as devotees. Omar wore a saffron kurta, blending in effortlessly. Afzal held a small prayer plate with incense, sweets and flowers. Inside the temple, the crowd was dense. Chanting filled the air, and the scent of camphor burned strong. But their eyes wandered beyond devotion.

They noted the layout - the main sanctum, the crowd management barriers, the side exits, the long boundary walls, and the towering old clock tower overlooking the inner compound. That structure, partially crumbling and seemingly ignored, caught their special interest.

"This tower is old," Omar whispered as they moved past it. "It's hollow inside. If we hide something there, no one will know."

Afzal nodded. "The bomb will need to be hidden during the night a day before the plan. We must study the guard routine. It's not just about hiding and ensuring it survives inspection."

They made several rounds of the temple, noting everything, how often the guards rotated shifts, the timing of the main crowd inflow, when the priests were busiest. They identified an alley behind the temple, one narrow and mostly used by sweepers, as their potential route of infiltration.

After spending the entire day in the temple premises, they left in the evening. Once they reached the dharmshala, they took out their laptop for the research in the temple. They found out how old it was, any special event planned in the mid of December and overall, approximately how many devotees came in a day to the temple.

The next day, it was time for exploring the rest of the area around the temple. Since most of the lanes reaching the temples were too narrow, it was potentially challenging for the backup team along with police or army jeeps, ambulances and other media to reach the premises on an urgent basis. They wanted the media coverage for the incident as soon as possible. If there was a delay in broadcast, it would delay the panic and the focus on the blast which would delay their main operation. Thus, they started exploring the alternate options available to reach there, and soon found one. It was a wide road leading to the temple main entrance. But they found a huge security checkpoint at the entrance of the lane, with no permission to enter.

They went to a vendor selling aarti plates, flowers and idols of Lord Shiva and asked him, "Does this road go to the temple?"

The vendor responded, "Yes! But you have to take the other way from the left side."

Omar further enquired, "Why? Is this closed? Any maintenance or construction going on?"

The vendor replied, "No, it is only meant for VIP vehicles entry. Whenever there are some politicians or any famous personality coming to the temple, they use this route. That is why there is much security on the road."

Both understood that during the incident, this would be accessible for emergency services and their concern for delayed coverage of the incident would be sorted out.

They moved ahead to find the closest police station. To their surprise, it was just next to the temple which they had missed noticing the day before. They noted the details, and moved ahead.

They spent another three days in Deoghar, blending into the crowd. During those days, they witnessed the morning and evening aarti, sat through crowded prayer sessions, and quietly mapped every blind spot.

At night, they discussed minute details in the confines of their room. The map Afzal sketched began to look more like a military blueprint. They marked security rounds and camera blind spots.

Afzal tapped his pen on the clock tower sketch. "We'll place the device in the central beam. If the top falls, it will collapse onto the sanctum. The destruction will be symbolic, not just physical."

Omar stared at the map, tracing the escape route. "The alley leads to the vegetable market. We'll change clothes, blend with vendors, and exit through the north gate by rickshaw."

Every hour they weren't sleeping, they were planning. They walked different streets every day, ensured they memorized routes and studied crowd movements by the hour.

When they finally left Deoghar, their minds were satisfied with the details of their requirements.

After completing the Deoghar plan, they were on a bus heading toward Bihar. The green fields of Jharkhand turned into the flat plains of Bihar as the bus neared Gaya. Their next stop was

Bodh Gaya, the sacred land where Gautama Buddha had attained enlightenment.

As the Mahabodhi Temple first appeared in the distance, Omar was struck by its serenity. The temple stood tall with its intricately carved spire and serene surroundings. Buddhist monks in maroon robes moved silently in meditation. Tourists from across the world had gathered, Japanese, Thai, Sri Lankan, and Western pilgrims. Security there was slightly tighter due to its international importance.

As usual, they looked for a low budget lodge and checked in keeping a low profile. This time, they decided to pose as spiritual seekers exploring religious harmony.

Unlike Deoghar, this temple complex was wide open but surrounded by high walls. Entry was restricted through metal detectors, and bags were checked. Every moment increased their concern as the security was way too tight and might risk the entire mission. They spent an entire day trying to find an alternate entry to the premises, but there was none. Omar told Afzal, "Getting the explosive inside the premises seems impossible here. There is way too much of security."

Afzal remained silent for a moment and then responded, "Yes! But we have to find an alternative. This is our most crucial target as we have maximum international tourists here. The entire elite security force will be here after the blast and it will be the top priority for the Indian government to cover and avoid further blasts. The Bagdogra Air Force team will be deployed to protect this area on priority."

Omar had already done some research on it and replied, "Bihta Air Force Station is closer from here and they might arrive earlier for protection."

Afzal noted the probability but was adamant of ticking a yes for the target. But they had to find some other plan.

They left for their lodge that day and back in their rooms, they thought of alternatives. They had only one solution, to find a loophole in the security team at the entrance. But that was way too risky and both Omar and Afzal weren't sure if the risk was worth taking as it may compromise the main mission. After discussions, when they didn't find any other alternative, they decided to go for it.

The next day, they stood out of the entrance a few metres away for the security check post and noticed that the security was handled by both CISF and local police. They got a loophole they were looking for. While they knew that breaking in the CISF security was impossible, the involvement of local police made it easy. They checked in the details of the local officers from police deployed at duty there through visual inspection, and noted who all were involved. Then they created a list containing 5 officers. They started finding out their background, their hometowns, family details and other personal information. Out of five two of them had their families in Gaya. One of the officers stayed with his joint family while the other stayed with his wife and a kid who was just three years old.

Both Omar and Afzal had the plan ready in their minds. Afzal narrated, "So, now we know our target. We will keep this officer's family hostage and through him, we will get into the premises. And we will get the work done."

Omar agreed to the plan. Then it was the time to check other details which they had checked for their previous targets.

They visited the temple daily for another three days, observing from different angles. The Bodhi tree, descendant of the original under which Buddha meditated, was fenced, but the fencing was symbolic. There were monks meditating just feet away, but no guards nearby.

Afzal pointed toward the tree. "We don't need to destroy the whole temple. A blast near the

Bodhi tree will be enough to send shockwaves across the world."

They walked the premises repeatedly, noting the positioning of cameras, the rhythm of security rounds, and the flow of tourists. They found a blind spot, a corner near the inner wall where the CCTV camera panned too slowly to offer real-time footage. It was there they planned to hide the device.

"Exit?" Omar asked.

"Through the south gate. We'll switch outfits in the public toilet nearby, merge into the tourist crowd, and take a bus from the Gaya stand."

They even visited nearby villages to scout potential hideouts for a few hours post-blast. They made note of a mango orchard where a local sympathizer owned a shed. That would be their refuge point.

Once they had completed inspecting Gaya, their journey took them to their fourth destination. Located in the state of West Bengal, Kharagpur was known not only for its vast railway station having one of the longest platforms in the country, but also as a key junction connecting major routes across India.

They arrived at Kharagpur Junction on a hazy afternoon. The air was filled with the sharp smell of engine grease and fried snacks from nearby stalls. Porters rushed past, balancing luggage on their heads, and announcements blared from loudspeakers in a blend of Bengali, Hindi, and English. The station was alive, chaotic, and enormous.

Afzal turned to Omar as they stepped onto the platform. "This isn't just a railway station. This is a lifeline. Cut this, and you slice through the nerves of eastern India."

They checked into a modest lodge near the station and started their work. Kharagpur station was an easier target as security check on railway stations weren't generally tight and getting on platforms was way too easy. Here the main target was to finds a location which had maximum impact. They also had the clarity that the location should be such that it blocks all railway movements which would disrupt the connectivity of eastern part of the country from rest of India.

They spent the first day at the station spending time on all the platforms. Since they had been on the station for more than 10 hours, a tea vendor noted this and got suspicious. He approached them ang asked, "Sir, do you have any problem or enquiry?"

Both Omar and Afzal were speechless for a while, but Omar acted completely normal and asked, "We have come from Jammu and come here for the first time. But we do not know which train to board to go to Kolkata. We are tourist and have come here yesterday."

The vendor got excited hearing Jammu and replied, "Wow! Jammu! I so much want to go to Vaishno Devi. Have you been there."

Omar continued, "Yes! It's very regular for us. We have our business there and we keep going."

The vendor asked, "You tell what help you need here?

Omar asked, "Will I get train for Kolkata from here?"

The vendor replied, "Yes! Of course. This is the biggest railway station. And main connection to Kolkata." Then he shared the train timings to him.

Afzal and Omar noted and moved away considering the fact that lot of questioning can create issues for them. They immediately left the station and went back to their hotel.

Once they were in their room, Afzal told, "It will be risky to go back to the station tomorrow. That vendor may be there again."

Omar nodded in agreement and said, "We will have to use the photographs we have taken today and find an appropriate spot."

The next day they used all the photographs, laid them on their bed in sequence and started observing. They plotted a map of the station with the major points like entrance, exits, ticket booking counters, enquiry counters, overbridges and the positioning of the Railway Protection Force (RPF) posts. They had figured their spot to hit.

"Place the device here," Afzal pointed to the sketch of the footbridge, "and it will kill hundreds. But more than that, it'll paralyze movement. No train will leave or arrive for hours, maybe days."

After that, it was time to explore nearby areas, but they had to be careful. They didn't want to be noticed or suspected as it happened last time. So, they decided to split and walk individually for smaller times in specific locations to avoid any suspicion.

They visited nearby workshops and maintenance yards, posing as mechanics scouting for jobs. Omar chatted with vendors, striking up conversations about schedules and shifts. They took mental notes of express train timings, checked for local police stations and routes to the nearest bus stand.

Then, they identified escape routes. Post-blast, the station would go into lockdown. Their plan involved slipping out through the abandoned side gate near the parcel office, blending with the labourers moving toward the market and from there to the bus stand. Their blueprint for Kharagpur was ready.

A month had passed in checking all four locations and it was time to check the India Nepal border which was the entrance point for their secondary team. They avoided staying in Bagdogra as the Army and Air Force personnel movement was very high and they could be suspected. They moved to Gangtok and took an SUV from there to reach the border directly.

They reached a small village near the border called Rhenock. From here, the duo moved carefully, posing as travel bloggers interested in documenting remote Himalayan trails. Their attire and cameras made the story believable.

For a couple of days, they walked along the routes frequented by local traders and nomads. The border area between India and Nepal was hardly demarcated by fencing for border marks in most places. There were mostly natural demarcations. There were dozens of unofficial trails crossing over into Nepal.

Omar made notes in a small journal while Afzal snapped photos discreetly. They were studying the rotation of Indian and Nepali patrols, how often soldiers passed, which checkpoints had dogs, and where the valleys provided natural cover.

They spoke with shepherds and tea vendors in the region. Many were sympathetic to anyone who opposed the Indian state. Some of them even pointed out areas where locals smuggled goods across the border without detection.

"See that bend," a shepherd told Omar. "You can walk through the riverbed there. Hardly any patrolling there."

For over a week, Omar and Afzal camped in makeshift tents, watched the stars from rocky ledges, and marked the sound of boots and vehicles. They counted Indian soldiers during day patrols, noted Nepalese Army's visibility, and calculated a timing window when neither side had surveillance.

"The best time is between 2:00 and 4:30 AM," Afzal said on the night when they were finally laying out the plan. "We can move through the forest trail near Tamor valley. No army surveillance and a strong support of natural shadows."

Omar nodded. "What about the cargo?"

"That's not a problem at all. There are several patches of dense forest which are completely unmanned and even villagers do not go there after sunset. We will use those routes during the night."

They finalized the plan with multiple crossings in a staggered manner. Once the team, disguised as shepherds, monks, or supply traders enter the country, from there, they would regroup deeper inside Indian territory near Siliguri.

"Once we breach this border," Afzal said, "India will be looking outward. But the fire will already be inside."

With border access planned, the final objective loomed on the horizon of Bagdogra Air Force Station and Northeast India.

The next morning, without wasting any time, Omar and Afzal left for Delhi. The journey was quiet, each lost in their own thoughts, focused on the next phase of their plan.

Upon reaching Delhi, Afzal guided Omar through a maze of narrow streets to an old, abandoned house. The structure stood in isolation, worn out and partially broken, clearly marked for demolition by the municipal corporation. The place was far from busy roads, and no one seemed to care about its existence anymore.

Afzal pointed towards the building. "This will be our storage space. I've checked thoroughly, there's no scheduled activity here for at least a year. We can safely use it for the next two months."

Omar looked around and nodded in approval. "This is perfect. We can store everything here without attracting any attention. Transporting materials within the country won't be a problem either."

Afzal turned to him and asked, "When is the material arriving?"

Omar replied calmly, "I visited Jama Masjid before we left Delhi. The contact who's responsible for supplying the explosives confirmed the handover for next week."

"Great," Afzal responded with a quiet sense of relief.

Omar added, "Once the consignment arrives, you'll need to receive it and secure everything here. I'll be leaving for the camp tomorrow. Movement has become more sensitive as surveillance at the border areas has increased, and it's becoming riskier with each passing day."

Afzal nodded slowly, understanding the seriousness of the situation.

The next morning, Omar quietly left for Srinagar. He knew the journey ahead would not be simple. To avoid detection, he would have to travel through unfamiliar paths, staying alert every moment.

Last Meet

Omar stood silently at the edge of the camp, eyes scanning the dusty horizon, heart pounding with anticipation. The mission he had been meticulously planning for the last three months, was finally about to be set into motion. Every detail, every conversation, every move had led to this moment. The camp was now buzzing with quiet intensity. He moved from one tent to another, shortlisting the names of those who would accompany him on this mission.

Omar didn't care much about who could shoot better or who had more combat training. For him, determination was the real strength. Skills could be taught, but unwavering belief in the cause was something that had to burn from within. He needed people who would not flinch, not doubt, even in the face of certain death.

After days of observing and testing, he finalized eight men. Two each would be assigned to four major locations for the coordinated bombings.

Omar himself would be present in Bagdogra, leading the operation there with the second team that would slip into India from the Nepal border, ready to act as per the plan.

The selected men were called together in a secluded corner of the camp. One by one, Omar met them, speaking to each, understanding their mindset. His presence was enough to ignite fire in their eyes. For them, Omar wasn't just a leader, he was an example, and the soul of their cause.

Meanwhile, far away in Delhi, Afzal had already received the explosives. He had moved them discreetly to the abandoned building, just as he and Omar had planned. Once the explosives were in place, Afzal began the next phase of arranging for mobile sim cards under fake identities, securing vehicles with forged number plates, and gathering outfits for each team member that would help them blend into local crowds. He made sure every little detail matched the look and feel of the area each team was assigned to.

Back in the camp, preparations were in full swing. The eight men chosen by Omar underwent an intense final stage of training. It wasn't just about how to assemble a bomb or avoid being traced, but more about keeping nerves steady, how to lie convincingly, and how to walk into a crowd and disappear like smoke.

The morning sun was just beginning to rise when a black SUV arrived at the camp, its tires raising a cloud of dust behind it. The door opened, and out stepped Zafar. The name alone was enough to bring stillness in the air. Omar stood to greet him with respect, and soon, the entire camp was lined up in silence.

Zafar looked at the team Omar had selected, his gaze sharp, piercing into each of their souls.

Then, standing tall, he addressed them with a voice that echoed across the valley.

"You all know what you're going for," he began. "You know the risks, the dangers, the price that might be asked from you. But you also know what's at stake. This mission is not just about bombs or deaths, it's about our future. A new future. A land where our people live without fear, where our families no longer have to bury their sons and daughters. A land free from the bloodshed caused by India."

He paused, letting his words sink in.

"You are the flame we have been preparing. You will set fire to the illusion of peace they pretend to have. And from those ashes, we will rise."

The team stood straighter. Their eyes showed no hesitation. They were ready to kill, ready to die, and above all, ready to be remembered.

After the speech, Zafar called Omar aside. They walked a short distance from the group. The air between them was filled with unspoken understanding.

"Today," Zafar said, "you are not just stepping into a mission, you are stepping into future. Don't forget why we started this. When we break the northeast from India, that land will be ours. A new country where we will live in peace. No more fear. No more death. No more waiting for justice. Our parents, our relatives, our friends, they will finally have their revenge through us."

Omar stood still, listening. When Zafar spoke of family, images flashed in his mind, images carefully planted during his brainwashing. His mother, lying in a pool of blood. His father's lifeless body. Soldiers walking over them, cold and unfeeling. The fire in him, once again, roared.

"I will ensure this mission is successful," Omar said, his voice steady and certain.

Zafar smiled. There was pride in his eyes. "I never doubted that. And that's why I have a gift for you. From my best soldier to my most trusted leader. Once our state is formed, you will lead its army."

The words struck Omar like lightning. Leading the army of a new country? It was more than he had ever imagined. A sense of honor filled him, pushing aside all fear.

"We will be successful," he said again, this time with deeper conviction.

That night, a grand dinner was organized. The open ground in the centre of the camp was lit with dim lights and surrounded by security. The team, usually treated as mere foot soldiers, now sat shoulder to shoulder with the top commanders, including Zafar himself. Plates of rich food were served including meat, bread, sweets, and tea. For once, they were not just soldiers, they were heroes.

After dinner, the time came. One by one, the team stood up and received final blessings from the seniors. Omar met Zafar one last time. Their handshake lingered, firm and meaningful.

Several jeeps waited on the outer edge of the camp with their engines running. The night was cold, the sky above full of stars. The air was still, as if the world itself was holding its breath.

Omar led his team into the jeeps. No one spoke during the journey. Each man was lost in his thoughts. Some prayed silently, others replayed the plan in their heads. Omar sat at the front, eyes forward, mind locked on the mission.

They didn't take the old route. The previous location had become too risky with army check posts, increased patrolling, and random checks. Instead, they chose the route Omar had used during his last infiltration crossing the stream much North to the regular route, followed by a narrow forest path, winding and unpredictable, and safer.

The jeeps stopped a few kilometres before the Line of Control. The rest of the journey had to be done on foot. Omar stepped down first and adjusted his backpack. The rest followed. In the darkness, under the cover of trees, Omar whispered, "Stay close. No mistakes from here on."

With quiet footsteps and steady hearts, they began the final part of their journey. The mission had begun.

Omar was extremely careful. With a big team under him, the chances of getting caught were high. Even a single mistake, even if one of them got caught, the whole mission could be in danger. Everything would collapse. So, every movement needed to be silent and swift.

They finally reached the border where they had to cross into Indian territory. Omar was fully alert. He expected army patrolling, checkpoints, and maybe hidden snipers keeping watch. He had warned his men in advance. "Stay low, don't rush, don't speak," he had instructed. He was prepared for a long halt in case they had to wait for the right moment.

But what he saw surprised him. The area, which usually had a tense air with army boots thumping the ground and jeeps patrolling around, looked completely abandoned. Not a single soldier in sight. No vehicles. No surveillance drones. The border looked like it had been forgotten by the Indian side. It was as if the government had given up control of this stretch, as if they no longer cared about what happened there. Omar stood still for a moment, scanning everything with suspicion.

"This is strange," he whispered.

He raised his hand slowly, signalling his team to stay behind while he moved ahead alone to check the area. He went around the trees, walked past the usual patrol paths, and even climbed up a small rock to look around. Still, there was no one. Not a single soul. It felt like a trap, but there was no sign of any setup either. No wires, no cameras, nothing.

"This can't be real," he thought.

Still, he was alert and prevented rushing. He ordered the team to move in small groups, leaving gaps between each group. Within an hour, they had crossed over and entered the nearby forest area on the Indian side. Omar led them to a dense forest where he had once taken shelter for a full day. It was the same place where he had hidden during a previous mission, and it had worked well then. He expected patrol jeeps to come around soon. So, they hid, waiting and watching.

Hours went by. Omar kept glancing toward the road, expecting dust clouds from an army vehicle or the echo of army boots. But none came. Not even a single jeep passed. No soldier on foot. No drone. It was too quiet.

Omar's eyes narrowed. "Why is there no one here?"

He was slightly delighted because it made their job easier. But it also gave rise to doubt in his mind. Could it be a trick? Or was something else going on? Maybe the Indian side was genuinely relaxed, or maybe they were planning something bigger.

But there was no time to dwell on it. The team had to move forward.

By late evening, they began the next leg of their journey. They moved through the forest paths, following a narrow trail toward Srinagar. As they approached the outskirts of the city by nightfall, things began to look more familiar. They finally started spotting signs of army presence. There were two check posts ahead and a few patrolling jeeps moving in a fixed route. That made Omar feel a little more normal again.

"It wasn't a trap," he thought. "They've just reduced their presence in the border area. Maybe because there has been no activity for long."

That theory made sense. If the army hadn't seen any cross-border movement or threats for almost a year, they might have had reduced the number of soldiers on duty. It looked like their enemy had fallen asleep.

By morning, they entered Srinagar, moving carefully through narrow lanes and back routes. Once inside the city, Omar divided the team.

"We cannot move as a group anymore," he said firmly. "The rest of the journey must be done individually."

He gave each member a time and location to meet in Delhi. The men nodded, understood the plan, and one by one, disappeared into the local markets. Some went toward the taxi stands, some boarded local buses, and others walked off in different directions. All of them were heading to Delhi, but in different ways, at different times, and on separate routes.

Omar, meanwhile, took another route. He went straight to Bashir's place. The moment Bashir saw Omar at his doorstep, he broke into a wide smile.

"Omar bhai! Finally! Where have you been?" he asked with genuine joy. "There's hardly any news about you these days. What are you up to?"

Omar entered and sat down, his body finally resting after a long and tense journey.

"I was in the camp, training the boys," he said calmly.

Bashir brought him water and then asked, with a look of concern, "There hasn't been any activity in the valley for months. The army thinks we've given up and we've vanished. What are we doing?"

Omar looked at him, and a cunning smile played on his lips.

"Let them think that," he said quietly. "It works in our favour. Probably that's why the check posts and patrolling on the border have gone down. They're not expecting anything now."

Bashir nodded slowly. "Yes, the army is definitely relaxed. The valley is open now. There's no fear. We can plan something deadly. Something big. This is the right time."

But Omar had already made up his mind.

"Well," he said. "I have a better plan. Much bigger than what you're thinking. But for now, I just came to check the ground reality. And your analysis."

Bashir leaned forward, sharing more updates.

"As I said," he began, "the army has cut down numbers. There's hardly any movement in the interior areas. They couldn't spot any of our boys for the last six months. At first, they were confused. But now, for the last two-three months, they've simply relaxed. The deployment is thinner. No more sudden raids. No intel missions. Nothing."

He paused, then asked with excitement, "So, shall we plan something big here? Shake them out of their sleep?"

"Relax, Bashir," said Omar, leaning back. "We will. And it will be something very big. Just wait. We'll show them who we really are."

Before leaving, Omar collected everything he needed. Detailed maps, army movement charts, troop numbers and patrol timings. Bashir had all of it, neatly recorded.

Once done, Omar left quietly and began his journey toward Delhi.

The next morning, the sky over Delhi was overcast, cloaked in a grey mist that hung low over the city like a silent omen. By mid-morning, all members of the team, had arrived in the capital.

They followed the location Omar had sent each of them while departing from Srinagar. Omar had decided not to head towards Afzal's residence. The risk was far too great. With so many of them speaking the dialect common in areas around the Line of Control in Kashmir, it was only a matter of time before someone would raise questions.

It was a narrow by-lane behind the crowded quarters near Jama Masjid, an area so chaotic, so densely packed with people, sounds, and smells, that even a dozen men moving together wouldn't attract attention. Street vendors shouted out their prices, scooter horns blared without pause, and the scent of kebabs mixed with incense filled the dusty air.

Each pair arrived separately, at staggered intervals. They passed unnoticed through the crowd, blending into the fabric of the city. From there, they walked maintaining small distance between them to the abandoned house where the explosives were hidden and one by one, they slipped into the house. The heavy wooden doors creaked open and closed without anyone watching.

Omar was already there, standing with Afzal near the corner of the large, dusty room. The walls were bare, except for the shadows of what once hung there. The only furniture was a broken wooden bench and a metal trunk resting in the far corner. A thick carpet of dust coated the floor, disturbed only by the footprints of those who had entered.

When the last man arrived, Omar looked around. His eyes were sharp, tired, but unwavering. He took a deep breath and stepped forward.

"This is the last time we all stand together," he said, his voice low but firm. "After this, the mission begins. If destiny is kind, we shall meet again, not in this land, but in our new country. And if we are destined to fall, then we'll meet in Jannat, my brothers."

A unified cheer filled the room, echoing off the walls. There was no fear in their eyes. Only fire.

Omar raised his hand for silence. "You all know your targets. Today is the 14th of December. In two days, on the 16th, at exactly 10 a.m., all four locations must be gone from the face of this earth. Howrah Bridge, Bodhi Tree in Bodh Gaya Temple, Baidyanath Temple, and Kharagpur Railway

Station. These are not just targets, they are symbols. And when they fall, the world will know what message we've sent."

He paused, letting the weight of his words sink in.

"After the execution, don't wait, don't look back. Head straight to Siliguri. By the time you get there, that land will already belong to us."

Afzal stepped forward then, holding a folder in his hand. His face was expressionless, but his voice carried urgency. "Remember what we told you. Every detail, the placement of the explosives, the exact time, the crowd flow, the surveillance zones, we've studied it all. Stick to the plan. One mistake can ruin everything. These areas will be under watch, so move like shadows."

Again, the men nodded. There was no room for error now. Each second had been mapped, each movement choreographed.

Omar moved toward the metal trunk in the corner. He opened it with a key that hung from his neck. Inside were several boxes, neatly sealed and wrapped in courier packaging. No one could have guessed what they held.

"These are your packages," he said. "Each one is prepared, rigged, and secured. They're disguised as parcels with fake shipping labels and barcodes. They'll pass through checks if you do your part right. Deliver them to the destination. Place them exactly where instructed. No improvisations."

One by one, each team stepped forward and received their package.

Afzal handed out small envelopes next. "These are your identities," he said. "Fake IDs, local addresses, regional names. Burn them after use. Don't carry anything on you that connects you to us, or to each other."

He pulled out another folder containing photographs of number plates. "These are the vehicles stationed near your targets. Parked in silent corners, engines cold, documents ready. Get to them once you arrive in your respective cities. Don't drive unless it's necessary. Stay unnoticed."

Lastly, he gave each team a basic mobile phone with a new SIM card. "Use these to contact only the assigned number. No personal calls, no messages, nothing else. We'll discard the numbers right after the operation."

The final instructions took over an hour, each detail recited with clinical precision. Then, as the sun began to lower over the dusty rooftops of old Delhi, the men split into pairs, silently leaving the haveli as quietly as they had entered.

They made their way to different railway stations across the city, Old Delhi, Nizamuddin, Anand Vihar, each team following separate routes.

They walked with torn cloth bags on their shoulders, the packages buried beneath layers of clothes and old blankets. Nothing about them looked unusual. They looked like labourers, students, pilgrims, just part of the everyday crowd moving through India's rail network.

In the train, the general compartments were already crowded. They squeezed in with the rest, standing shoulder to shoulder with tired farmers, crying babies, old men clutching newspapers. No one suspected a thing.

The trains began to move, each one inching its way out of the capital like veins spreading out across the body of the country. The sound of wheels grinding against tracks was lost in the chaos. Inside, the men sat silently, their eyes steady, minds already focused on the next two days.

Destination

The groups had finally reached their assigned destinations, each scattered across with a single goal in mind. The team designated for Bodh Gaya had first travelled by train till Patna Junction. From Patna, they boarded a local state transport bus that was packed with daily commuters, villagers, and pilgrims.

The bus dropped them off near Gaya station. The team didn't waste time and quickly hired a local auto rickshaw. The auto pulled up outside the revered Mahabodhi Temple. Just a few metres away stood a small line of budget lodges catering to pilgrims. The group chose one with minimal attention, a small two-storey structure with a dimly lit reception. They booked a room for two days under fake names and spent the rest of the day inside, silently preparing for the next morning.

As the first rays of the sun fell over the sacred temple and the bells echoed through the air, the group woke up. They dressed simply like tourists, blending in with the morning crowd. Abdul, the man in charge of this leg of the operation, checked the package one last time.

By 7:30 am, Abdul and his companion quietly slipped out of the lodge and took a longer route through less crowded streets, avoiding the main road. After about a 15-minute walk, they arrived in front of a modest government quarter, the residence of a local police officer stationed at the temple. They stood outside the gate for a moment, carefully scanning their surroundings.

Ensuring that no one was looking at them, Abdul knocked on the door firmly. A few seconds later, a woman, likely in her mid-thirties, opened the door slightly. She peeped through the half opened door, puzzled.

"Who are you?" she asked.

"There is a parcel for sir. Is he available?" Abdul asked, holding up the box.

The woman looked at the parcel and replied casually, "He's on duty. I am his wife. You can hand it over to me."

That was the confirmation they needed. Abdul and his companion swiftly pushed the complete door open. She gasped, trying to scream, but it was too late. Abdul was quick to clamp his hand over her mouth while his companion held her arms. The struggle didn't last more than a few seconds. Abdul pulled out a small cloth soaked in local anaesthesia and pressed it to her nose. She squirmed, tried to resist, but soon her eyes rolled back and she collapsed onto the floor, unconscious.

"Quick, check the house," Abdul instructed.

His partner rushed inside. One of the rooms had a child, no older than three, fast asleep under a mosquito net. The man stepped in silently, pulled out another cloth, and held it gently over the child's nose. The boy stirred for a moment, but within seconds, he too was unconscious, lying limp on the bed.

They dragged the woman inside and laid her beside the child. Abdul took a moment to ensure they were both breathing and unharmed, just sedated.

Then, he pulled out a small phone and made a crucial call.

On the other end, the officer answered groggily, not expecting a call from an unknown number so early.

Abdul's voice was calm but laced with menace. "Your wife and child are with us. They're safe... for now. I don't want money or anything else. All I want is your help getting inside the Bodh Gaya temple without any security checks. I'll meet you at 8:00 am outside the main gate. No ifs. No buts. Do what I say… or forget you ever had a family."

There was silence.

Then, a shaky voice responded, "What… What do you mean? Who are you?"

But Abdul had already ended the call.

Back at the temple, the officer stood frozen. His hands were trembling. Sweat poured down his forehead even in the morning chill. Thoughts swirled through his mind whether was this a bluff? Was his family really in danger? But the fear in his chest told him it wasn't a prank. He couldn't afford to take that risk. By the time he could think of taking any action, Abdul arrived at the temple gate. He was dressed simply, carrying a bag. His eyes scanned the area and locked onto the officer.

"You've made the right choice by showing up," Abdul said calmly, approaching him.

The officer's face was pale, his lips dry.

"My partner is still at your house. He has explosives. If he senses anything unusual, a single cop trying to be a hero, your entire block will be gone," Abdul warned.

To make his point, he slightly unzipped his bag and revealed a portion of the actual explosive he was carrying. The officer stepped back instinctively.

"I just want to get inside without a check. That's it. You help me, and your family stays safe. Simple," Abdul added.

The officer didn't say anything. He just nodded slowly.

"Take me through the staff entry. Somewhere discreet."

The officer turned and began walking through a narrow alley that led to a side entrance, one used occasionally by staff and maintenance workers. A few fellow officers were present, but he managed a convincing smile and waved.

"This is my relative from Jammu," the officer said casually. "Just giving him a quick tour."

No one suspected anything. The reputation of the officer, combined with the early hour and the regular flow of people, worked in Abdul's favour. Soon, they were inside the temple complex, a peaceful haven of prayer and silence.

Abdul leaned in close and said, "You will stay with me till 10:00 am. After that, you're free to go."

The officer looked around. Every fibre of his being was screaming to alert someone, to stop this madman. But the image of his unconscious wife and child haunted his thoughts. He nodded again.

The officer, still in dilemma, knew that something very damaging was to happen. Abdul too knew that if the officer alerted anyone from the police or CISF team, the mission would be compromised.

"I need to use the washroom. Somewhere quiet," Abdul said.

The officer hesitated. "There's one near the rear side. Not used much."

"Perfect."

They walked there quietly, and once they reached, the officer gestured towards the small facility. As he turned to leave, Abdul moved swiftly. He grabbed the officer from behind, held the same anaesthesia cloth to his face, and within seconds, the man dropped, unconscious.

Abdul dragged him into a cubicle, sat him on the commode like someone using it, and locked the door from inside. Then, he climbed over the partition wall and jumped down, alone now in the temple premises.

The explosive bag was with him. He walked slowly through the temple grounds, blending in with the early pilgrims. The chants of monks filled the air. A faint fragrance of incense lingered everywhere. People were praying under the sacred Bodhi tree.

He made his way there silently, found a supporting pillar not too far from the tree, and casually sat beside it. In a few quiet minutes, he carefully unzipped the bag and placed the device behind the pillar, hidden from plain sight. All he had to do was wait for another thirty minutes. Then, chaos would begin.

Meanwhile, hundreds of miles away from the sacred silence of Bodh Gaya, another group had already reached their target location, the majestic

Howrah Bridge of Kolkata, a night before the bombing. Their task was as critical, if not more. Unlike the subtle, silent placement of a bomb in a temple, their job was a little tricky. The bomb they carried was designed to bring down a steel giant, to send shockwaves across the nation.

Their train pulled into Howrah Station a little after 10:00 pm. Even at that hour, the station was bustling with porters shouting, passengers dragging luggage, announcements echoing overhead in three languages. The night air was heavy with humidity with a faint smell of fish from nearby stalls.

But the two men, Altaf and Iqbal, kept their heads down, avoiding eye contact, speaking in low tones. They carried one backpack each, sturdy, dusty bags that could easily pass for those of tired travelers. But only one of those contained the payload that would change the skyline of Kolkata by the next day.

Once they were out of the station, they could see the majestic outline of Howrah Bridge standing like a silver skeleton in the night sky. Towering over the Hooghly River, lit by sparse yellow street lamps, the steel beams shimmered slightly under the moonlight. It stood proud and strong, as it had for decades, connecting the twin cities of Howrah and Kolkata.

Their eyes locked onto it like predators on a target. But they knew better than to act immediately. The bridge might look peaceful from a distance, but even at night, there was traffic, a few trucks, late-night taxis, and pedestrians still trickling through. Their window of action would be narrow, very narrow.

They crossed the road and entered a small local eatery tucked into a side alley. The place was modest, with wooden benches, dim yellow lights, and a cracked television playing an old Bengali movie. They sat quietly in a corner and ordered what most others were eating, fish curry with rice, along with a glass of water. Every now and then, they glanced at the clock on the wall.

11:30 pm.

They ate slowly, cleaned their hands, paid in cash, and stepped out into the night again. The streets were growing quieter. A cool breeze blew in from the river, bringing with it the sound of occasional honking and distant ferry horns. They walked towards the bridge, trying to look like casual pedestrians heading home late.

By midnight, the traffic on Howrah Bridge had thinned out. Most of the vendors had packed up. Only a few random vehicles crossed every five to ten minutes. This was the silence they had been waiting for.

They looked at each other once. No words were spoken. Both men began walking toward the centre of the bridge. The river below glistened like ink under the moonlight, and the steel beams stretched above them like a massive skeleton of iron bones.

As they reached the central portion, they slowed down. They scanned their surroundings to ensure no pedestrians, no cops, no beggars hiding in corners. Just the sound of the river beneath and the occasional rumble of a truck far away on either end.

That was it.

One by one, they climbed over the side railing, the river-facing barrier of the bridge. Gripping tightly onto the steel beams for balance, they maneuvered themselves to the outer edge. It was risky, one wrong step, and they would plunge straight into the Hooghly, swept away by its dark waters.

But they were trained and remained focused. Slowly, with silent determination, they began to climb downward along the steel beams. Their boots found footing on narrow metal bars, their hands gripping tightly as they moved lower and lower, inch by inch. The wind was stronger underneath, whistling through the iron lattice, and the faint vibrations of vehicles above pulsed through the steel.

They finally reached the underside of the bridge to find the massive network of cross beams, supports, and hollow panels that held the entire structure together. It was dark and damp, with small patches of moss growing on some parts. Bats fluttered in the corners, disturbed by their presence.

Iqbal unzipped his backpack to pull out the explosive device. It was large, larger than the one placed in Bodh Gaya, about the size of a small suitcase, and carefully sealed. Wires coiled inside the casing, still covered with protective cloth. This wasn't something one picked off a market shelf, it had been custom-made, powerful enough to compromise structural integrity.

"Hold the beam steady," Iqbal whispered.

Altaf nodded and used both arms to stabilize one of the diagonal support pillars that connected two larger cross-sections. Iqbal then placed the device against the steel pillar that ran horizontally beneath the centre of the bridge. It was slightly elevated, a critical load-bearing beam.

They took out industrial-strength adhesive strips, metal clamps, and wire hooks to fasten the bomb tightly. They didn't want it sliding down or falling into the river. The adhesive stuck almost instantly, bonding the explosive casing with the steel.

Iqbal tightened the clamps and gave it a slight tug. It didn't move.

"Perfect," he muttered.

It was time to climb back up. They carefully turned, using the beams like ladders, climbing inch by inch, pausing every time they heard the faint growl of an engine or a headlight beam sweeping across the bridge. Halfway up, they pressed themselves flat against the metal, hiding from a passing cab whose headlights briefly lit up the steel maze.

Once the vehicle passed, they resumed climbing. Their hands were grimy, shirts soaked in sweat, but their focus never wavered. After several breathless minutes, they reached the side railing again. They crouched low, waiting for another empty moment in traffic. A single motorbike passed, then a lull.

"Now," Altaf whispered.

Both swung one leg over the railing, then the other, and landed softly on the sidewalk of the bridge. They adjusted their clothes, dusted off their hands, and began walking casually, not too fast, not too slow.

They headed straight to a cheap lodge near the station, the kind with flickering tube lights, damp-smelling beds, and a front desk clerk too sleepy to care who checked in. They gave false names, paid in cash, and were handed keys to a room on the first floor.

Inside, they locked the door, drew the curtains, and lay down on their respective beds. Neither spoke a word for a while.

The bridge was set. All they had to do was wait.

The town of Deoghar woke slowly, wrapped in the early morning haze that hung low over its narrow streets and old temples. Faint temple bells rang from somewhere in the distance, announcing the break of dawn. The shops were still closed, shutters pulled down, and only the occasional chai vendor had started setting up his stall near the railway station.

Two men, Haider and Bilal, stepped off the train just as the first light of the morning touched the sky. It was around 4:30 am. Their train had arrived from Ranchi, a less obvious route, meant to avoid suspicion. The two had travelled light. Each carried a small backpack and wore regular cotton kurtas, blending in effortlessly with the stream of pilgrims and early travelers. They moved swiftly past sleepy rickshaw pullers and stray dogs curled by the walls. They didn't speak much. A nod here, a glance there, their language was silent.

Outside the station, they hailed a cycle-rickshaw.

"Mandir," Bilal said softly.

The rickshaw-puller didn't ask questions. He just adjusted the shawl over his shoulder and began pedalling through the empty roads, the old wheels creaking quietly over the asphalt.

By 5:00 am, they had reached the temple. The Baidyanath Temple stood like a monument frozen in time. Its white shikhara towered above the nearby buildings, stained over the years by soot, rain, and millions of incense sticks offered by the faithful. The streets near the temple complex were beginning to stir. A few devotees had already arrived, some sleeping on the sidewalks, others bathing at nearby water taps.

The duo paid the rickshaw-puller and walked to a narrow alley just behind the temple complex. It was lined with small lodges and dharmshalas. They checked into a dimly lit one, giving false names and IDs. The sleepy receptionist barely looked at them before handing over a key to a room on the ground floor. They entered, bolted the door, and sat in silence.

Bilal opened his bag. Inside, beneath a layer of folded clothes, was the device. It was compact, metallic, and carefully packed in a pressure-locked box. The detonating device was already wired, all that remained was to plant it at the right place and arm it. The explosion was to be triggered at 10:00 am sharp, the same timeline as the others.

At 6:00 am, the temple gates officially opened. The loud conch shells began to echo across the town. Hundreds of people had already begun to pour in, men with wet dhotis, women in bright sarees, children holding their parents' hands.

Haider looked at Bilal and gave a slight nod. It was time.

They changed into devotee attire, simple white dhotis and cotton scarves around their necks. Haider applied a bit of sandalwood paste on his forehead, bought from a nearby vendor. Bilal carried a brass lota filled with water from the sacred

Shiv Ganga Kund, which he had collected earlier in the morning, just like every other pilgrim did before entering the temple.

They joined the line of devotees moving towards the temple gates. CISF personnel were managing the queues, but the checks were quick, and the volunteers were too few. With so many people pushing forward, the guards only had time to do surface-level frisking.

Their device was hidden in a separate pouch sewn inside Bilal's dhoti, tightly strapped to his thigh. The casing was slim, curved to contour with his body, and wrapped in protective cloth. Since there was no metal detector and only hand frisking, there was no concern for Bilal and Haider. They walked slowly, mimicking the other barefooted devotees with their hands folded in prayer.

Inside the temple, the energy was electric. People chanted "Har Har Mahadev!" in waves, the sound bouncing off the stone walls of the thousand-year-old complex. The scent of incense and ghee filled the air, mixing with sweat, flowers, and wet cloth.

The main temple structure stood tall, the central sanctum where the Jyotirlinga was housed. A long queue of devotees snaked around the inner courtyard, waiting for darshan. Haider and Bilal did not join that line. Instead, they moved around to the backside of the complex, an area that few visited, with a narrow-shaded corridor and old stone pillars that had seen centuries pass.

This was the spot they had chosen.

One of the small, weathered walls close to the base of the main temple provided a blind spot, away from the cameras and out of the line of sight of most guards. This was the location described by Omar in the plan shared with both.

Bilal leaned down, pretending to adjust the knot of his dhoti. As he bent, Haider shielded him with his body, pretending to take a sip from the brass lota. At that moment, Bilal unfastened the strap, took out the explosive wrapped in a cloth soaked with temple ash and vermillion to blend in, and carefully wedged it between two loose stones at the base of the pillar.

The structure was old. The stones were uneven, with gaps perfect for hiding the small device.

The two then merged back with the crowd, joining a group of pilgrims sitting under a shaded mandap. They chanted with them, sipped tea from plastic cups handed out by temple volunteers, and even took part in the offering rituals. The minutes crawled forward.

By 9:00 am, the temple complex was bursting with people. Lines extended outside the gates.

Haider and Bilal kept low profiles, moving from one shaded corridor to another, always staying near exits. They had already identified their escape route, a side gate used by temple staff that opened onto a narrow alley leading back toward their lodge.

At 9:15 am, Bilal whispered, "Thirty minutes more. We leave at quarter to ten and move to the next premises."

Haider nodded.

They stood in the shadow of the bell tower, pretending to admire the temple's carvings. A few families gathered nearby, a photographer taking group pictures with the temple in the background. No one paid attention to the two men.

At 9:45 am sharp, the duo quietly slipped out through the side gate and waiting outside the main gate. They were in reach to ensure the detonator worked from the distance they were standing. The guards posted there didn't notice anything odd, people were coming and going constantly. The morning bells rang louder than ever. Devotees continued to chant, unaware of the ticking clock embedded deep in the temple's ancient stones.

The long-distance train rolled into Kharagpur Railway Station a little after midnight. The platform buzzed with activity, even at that odd hour. Vendors still shouted for tea, sleepy passengers disembarked with yawns, and coolies hovered near the staircases waiting for their next customer.

Among the sea of tired travelers, two men stepped onto Platform 3. They looked no different from the others with modest backpacks, cotton shirts clinging to their backs with sweat, and expressions that showed the fatigue of long travel. But unlike the others, they had no destination beyond the station. They were already there.

The taller one was Moshin. The other, leaner, slightly hunched, was Rafiq. Both had arrived from Jamshedpur, using unreserved tickets to avoid leaving a trace of their names in any manifest.

Omar had clearly briefed the mission to both to plant the explosive on the main walk-over bridge that connected all platforms. It was a bridge used by thousands of passengers every single day. The blast, if timed right, would bring down the central structure and rain chaos onto the tracks below. The time for detonation was synchronized with the rest of the locations.

The bridge was massive, an iron skeleton painted in faded blue and rust, stretching from Platform 1 to Platform 7. Trains passed underneath it every few minutes. People used it constantly in waves and bursts, carrying luggage from one platform to another. There was never a time when it was truly empty.

But Moshin and Rafiq had a plan. They loitered near the staircase of Platform 4, pretending to wait for someone. A security guard passed by, barely glancing at them. Rafiq leaned against a pillar, watching the rhythm of the crowd. Moshin bought a cup of tea from a vendor nearby. The clock ticked to 1:00 am.

They needed the bridge to be near-empty with just a small window of three to five minutes when no one was looking. And at 2:00 am, that time finally arrived.

A goods train had just thundered through. One express train was about to arrive on Platform 6, and another was delayed by thirty minutes. There was a short lull.

The duo began to move. They climbed the stairs slowly, like any other tired traveller. On the bridge, the lights flickered faintly overhead. A single sweeper, a woman with a long broom, was working her way toward the far end. A couple of railway police officers were crossing through the bridge, chatting lazily and sipping chai. Nothing unusual.

Moshin walked to the middle of the bridge and leaned on the railing, pretending to look at the trains below. Rafiq joined him, keeping his bag on the ground and squatting beside it like he was searching for something inside.

Inside Rafiq's bag was the device shaped like a lunchbox, painted black, and rigged with a remote-controlled detonator. The outer casing was disguised with a layer of foil and plastic, meant to look like a parcel wrapped in plastic.

Moshin kept his eyes on the patrol officers, watching for any sudden movement. Rafiq opened a side zip and slid the device out, keeping it close to his body. He moved to the side beam of the bridge where a thick, hollow metal pillar was connected vertically to the bridge floor. The area under the metal grill was rarely checked, filled with cobwebs, old chewing gum, and the grime of decades.

Quickly and silently, Rafiq knelt and unscrewed the bolts on the maintenance cover using a custom-made magnetic key. The panel popped open with a faint *click*. He reached inside the beam, wedged it between the inner metal supports and fastened the bomb using a strong adhesive gel. The device was concealed perfectly and nothing was visible from outside.

The whole act took less than sixty seconds. When Rafiq rose, he wiped his hands on his shirt and zipped the bag again. Moshin turned, gave a brief look down the bridge to confirm no one had seen. The sweeper was still at the far end. The officers were now standing, laughing about something and paying no attention.

They walked down the stairs to Platform 1 without drawing the slightest attention.

The job was done. They moved toward a public washroom and cleaned up. Rafiq checked the remote detonator in his pocket to ensure it was armed.

By 3:00 am, they left the platform area and exited the station through the side gate near the bus stand. The streets outside were empty. A few auto-rickshaws were parked near a tea shop that had just begun preparing its first kettle for the day. They walked past them and entered a small lane behind the market, where they booked a room at a cheap lodge under fake names.

Inside the room, Moshin took off his shirt and lay on the bed. Rafiq stood near the window, watching the stars vanish as the sky slowly turned silver with the approaching dawn. They didn't talk about what they had done. There was no pride, no emotion. Just silence and the ticking of the clock.

At 6:00 am, Kharagpur Station came to life.

Trains began arriving every fifteen minutes. Platforms filled with vendors shouting over one another, families shouting for porters, announcements echoing constantly.

The walk-over bridge was now packed.

By 8:00 am, it had become a river of people with office-goers, hawkers with head baskets, and hundreds of travellers rushing to catch their morning trains. None of them knew that the very structure beneath their feet carried a deadly secret.

At 9:00 am, Moshin and Rafiq left the lodge. They checked out without a word and walked to Platform number 1 of the railway station. They walked near the foot-over bridge and stood on a close proximity to ensure the detonator connects with the bomb and works. They just had to wait for 10:00 am.

Turning Point

The dusty room of the roadside lodge near the Bagdogra Air Force Station was dimly lit. A humming pedestal fan lazily spun above, doing little to cut through the thick April heat. Omar and Afzal sat on either side of a small wooden table, their backs straight, eyes fixed on the television screen. The walls around them were bare except for an old wall clock, ticking steadily towards ten.

They were dressed like tourists, Afzal wore a pair of faded jeans and a loose jacket, while Omar had draped a scarf around his neck, masking the sharpness of his features. A pair of hiking bags sat beside the bed, filled not with maps or supplies, but weapons and tactical gear. They were calm, unnervingly calm.

They had received encrypted confirmations early morning from all four teams - Bodh Gaya, Howrah, Deoghar, and Kharagpur. The bombs were in place, timers synced, exits mapped. All that was left now was the final signal of the explosion itself. And for that, there would be no phones, no calls, no digital traces. Only the news would tell them what they needed to know.

10:00 AM.

Afzal's fingers tapped the table lightly. Omar stared straight ahead, his jaw clenched. The TV anchor was mid-sentence when the broadcast was interrupted by a red ticker flashing across the screen.

"BREAKING NEWS: Multiple blasts reported across Eastern India. Details emerging."

Afzal's eyes widened. The channel quickly switched to a live feed showing chaos at Howrah Bridge, thick smoke rising above the city skyline. Another image cut to Bodh Gaya, sirens wailing, people running. Deoghar's serene temple town was now a vision of panic. Similar was the scene at Kharagpur Railway Station. The plan had worked. The clockwork had ticked in their favour.

Omar let out a slow breath. He looked at Afzal, and both shared a single nod, a quiet moment of victory.

"No phones. I'll do it," Omar said, pulling out a small radio transmitter. He tapped in a short-coded message, and within seconds, it was received by the secondary team waiting on the Nepal side of the border.

About sixty kilometres away, a group of six men emerged from the thick Sal Forest near the India-Nepal border. Clad in civilian clothes and carrying backpacks, they blended easily with the regular cross-border traffic.

Each of them carried modified rifles, grenades, and enough ammunition to sustain a short battle. The confirmation had reached them that phase one was a success. Now, Bagdogra was in their sights.

The men moved swiftly, boarding a small vehicle that had been left for them just outside the forest. It was a plain white SUV with a fake West Bengal number plate. Within an hour, they crossed Islampur and entered the outskirts of Siliguri, steering towards the southern approach of Bagdogra.

Meanwhile, inside the Air Force Station, all hell had broken loose.

Sirens had blared within minutes of the news breaking. Orders were being screamed into radios. Officers in fatigues dashed through corridors. Fighter jets were prepped and pushed onto the runway, ready to be airborne. The eastern command had immediately ordered aerial surveillance of the attacked zones, and air support was being dispatched. Helicopters chopped into the sky, rising above the base with urgency.

That was precisely what Omar wanted, a perfect distraction. With the main forces and attention pulled towards the blast locations, Bagdogra's secondary entrance had minimal protection.

By 11:15 AM, the team from Nepal arrived at the rendezvous point, an abandoned irrigation house located about 500 meters from the Air Force Station's lesser-used gate on the northern side. Omar and Afzal were already there, seated on a fallen log under the cover of thick trees. They stood as the vehicle came into view.

Afzal stepped forward and quickly signaled. One by one, the six men got out. Omar scanned them, tired, dust-covered, but ready.

"Everything set?" one of them asked, adjusting the strap on his rifle.

"More than ready," Omar replied. "Weapons are here. Targets are marked."

They opened their bags and pulled out AK47s, rocket launchers, and grenades. Omar handed out small communication devices.

"The goal is simple," he said. "We take the secondary gate. We block the runway. No flights. No escape. Once that's done, we secure the barracks near the northwest wall and hold our ground. Reinforcements from the base have already moved out. That gives us time."

They moved with purpose, crouching low as they approached the forest edge. The station was partially visible from there, a long wire fence marked the perimeter, guarded by sporadic patrols. The main entrance, they knew, would be under strict surveillance now. But this entrance, which was less used, partially hidden behind storage units and fuel tanks, was their window.

The sound of fighter jets roared above them, one after the other. The airspace was alive. From their vantage point, Omar could see the smoke trails of aircrafts rising fast.

"This is it," he whispered to Afzal. "They've sent most of their birds. Bagdogra is light now."

Afzal nodded. "We hit them hard. And we don't stop."

They split into three units, two men positioned with long-range rifles near the trees, tasked with covering fire. The rest advanced stealthily, keeping to the shadows of storage units and fencing. Omar led from the front.

The entrance gate loomed ahead. It was sturdier than they anticipated. It was heavily guarded, much more than usual after the incident. The plan was to go in silence, but Omar had prepared for all outcomes.

He turned to the group and held up three fingers. His voice dropped to a whisper, barely audible.

"This is the time we've all been waiting for. We're not here to retreat. We move forward. We take control."

The dry wind of the plain whipped past Omar's face as he crouched silently behind the broken wall of the abandoned shed. His breathing was steady, eyes sharp, ears tuned to every rustle in the air. It was the final stretch of their most critical mission. Everything had gone according to plan until then.

He lifted his arm to give the signal. His fingers tightened to make the countdown—three... two...

But before he could even count one, a sudden loud crack shattered the silence, a bullet had been fired. The sound was so close, it echoed in his ears. Instinctively, he turned to his right, trying to locate the source.

And what he saw froze the breath in his lungs.

Afzal, the man who had stood beside him through countless operations, was lying motionless on the ground. His eyes were wide open, staring blankly into the sky, as a dark red patch spread across his chest. Omar's heart skipped a beat.

Before the shock could even register properly, a second shot rang out. Then a third. Then a fourth. And it continued—sharp, ruthless, unforgiving.

Omar looked around in disbelief, his instincts screaming at him to move, to fight, to do something, but all he could do was watch. One by one, his men dropped to the ground like dominoes, each life extinguished in a matter of seconds. His entire team, his carefully chosen, highly trained team, was wiped out.

He couldn't understand what was happening. How? How could this be possible?

He had planned every step of the mission with utmost secrecy. No phone calls. No written plans. No digital footprints. Meetings were held face-to-face, in hidden places, always on the move. He'd taken every measure to stay invisible. Then how?

Who knew?

And who were *they*?

He couldn't see anyone. No movement in the grass. No shadows in the trees. Just his men lying dead, and the gunshots that came from nowhere.

Then, without warning, pain exploded through his arm.

A bullet tore through his right bicep, ripping apart the muscle and sending a jolt of agony through his body. His rifle slipped from his hands and crashed to the dry ground. Blood gushed out of his wound and soaked into the soil beneath him. The heat of it, the smell of it, the sight of it, it was all too real. Before he could gather himself, another shot, this time the aim was his knees and his calf muscle tore apart. His knees gave way, and he fell.

He tried to crawl, to drag himself behind some cover, but his body felt too heavy, too distant. The pain was overwhelming, and with each second, he could feel the strength draining from his wounded parts.

He lay there, gasping, his face half-buried in the dust, eyes fluttering open and shut. The warm trickle of blood continued to spill from his arm and leg, and he could feel the earth drinking it up greedily. The sound of gunfire had stopped now, replaced by a strange, eerie silence. Even the birds had gone quiet.

And then, in the haze of pain and confusion, he saw them.

Two figures, silhouettes at first, walking slowly toward him.

Dressed entirely in black. From head to toe, black uniforms, black boots, black gloves, black masks that covered their faces. They held sleek rifles in their hands, steady and firm. They moved with precision, calm and deliberate, like trained shadows.

Omar blinked. His vision was blurring. He tried to lift his head, to focus, but the blood loss was too much. He could feel his consciousness slipping away.

Who were these men?

How had they found them?

Were they soldiers? Commandos? Or someone else?

A part of him wanted to scream, to shout for help, but his throat was dry and no sound came out. He could feel his body growing colder, his limbs becoming numb. His eyelids felt like they weighed a hundred pounds.

He tried to hold on, to stay awake, to get at least one clear look at them. But his eyes had other plans.

The last thing he saw before darkness claimed him was the barrel of a rifle pointed directly at him and the faint glint of the sun reflecting off a silver insignia on one of their shoulders.

A pale white ceiling blurred above him. The hum of machines, a sharp antiseptic smell, and the soft beeping of a monitor filled the stillness. Omar's eyelids fluttered open slowly. His throat was dry. His body ached all over, and his head throbbed like a drum. He tried to move, but a sharp sting in his left wrist stopped him.

His eyes moved to the side.

A steel handcuff clamped his left hand to the iron railing of the hospital bed. An oxygen mask was strapped to his face. An IV needle was pricked into his left hand, and bandages covered most of the upper arm of the right hand, where the bullet had pierced him.

The room was quiet.

Opposite to him, near the door, stood a nurse dressed in military green scrubs. She was flipping through some papers on a clipboard, glancing at him from the corner of her eye. When she noticed Omar's eyes were open and moving, she immediately placed the file aside and walked out of the room in a hurry.

Moments later, the door opened again. This time, a group entered including a couple of doctors in white coats, two army officers in olive green uniforms and a man in a navy-blue formal suit with a stiff expression and deep, calculating eyes.

One of the doctors stepped forward and checked the monitors, then touched Omar's forehead, gently pulled down the lower eyelids, and finally gave a nod.

"He's conscious. The sedation has worn off. You can move him tomorrow morning," the doctor announced, speaking to the army officers without even looking back at Omar.

Omar didn't say a word. His throat was parched, and he had no strength to speak. But his mind was slowly piecing together what had happened.

He had been shot. His men, Afzal and the entire squad were dead. He had bled, passed out. Now there he was, alive, but caught.

Captured.

The army had taken him.

That was not an ordinary hospital. It was a military hospital, clean, efficient, silent, guarded. And soon, they would come for answers. They would ask questions about his operations, about the attacks he'd planned, the men he trained, the routes they took, the contacts they had, the foreign handlers and every other detail he had. The entire information hidden in his brain would be pulled out.

And if he didn't speak, they had other ways of making him talk.

The next morning, under heavy security, Omar was transferred to a military establishment on the outskirts of the city. It was a concrete structure, old and cold, with a high wall and barbed wire fencing all around. Armed guards stood at every corner. Cameras watched every move.

He was taken through narrow corridors into a room with no windows, a single table, three chairs, and yellow bulb at one end of the room. On the wall behind him was a giant mirror, he knew it was a one-way glass. People were watching from the other side.

Inside, three men waited. Two officers in uniform, both in their late thirties, stern-faced and composed. The third man, same person from the hospital, wore a formal suit, a senior intelligence officer, no doubt.

Omar was made to sit. His hands were cuffed to a metal loop fixed into the table.

They offered him water. Then, without raising their voices or throwing threats, they began.

The questions came slowly, softly.

"Who was your handler in Nepal?"

"How did you cross the border?"

"Who provided the RDX for the blasts?"

"Which group was supposed to attack Bagdogra?"

"What was your communication method?"

"Where is the next cell based?"

And the most important question, "Who else apart from Zafar was involved in this?"

Hearing Zafar's name, Omar realized the army and intelligence already had a decent detail of the attack.

Hours passed.

At first, Omar resisted. He remained silent, trying to appear defiant. But the fatigue in his body and the pain in his arm were too real. And the tone of the men questioning him wasn't angry or violent, it was confident, too confident.

They already knew most of the answers.

Every time Omar lied, they corrected him.

Every time he hesitated, they filled in the blank.

Eventually, the resistance began to crack.

Piece by piece, he started confessing. First reluctantly. Then with frustration. Then in a desperate tone, as if trying to justify himself.

He told them about the meetings in the camps, the training in the mountains, the routes they used to enter India. He described the planning, how four different teams were assigned to bomb different locations, Bodh Gaya, Baidyanath

Temple, Howrah Bridge, and the upcoming plan at Bagdogra Air Force Station. He even explained how he stayed underground, how he misled the intelligence agencies.

When he finished, he leaned back in the chair, exhausted but with a faint flicker of pride in his eyes.

"I managed to carry out the biggest synchronized bombings in the country," he said, looking directly at the suited officer.

But instead of the reaction he expected, panic, disbelief, even anger, something strange happened.

The officer smiled.

Then he chuckled.

And then both army officers began to laugh, quiet at first, then louder, shaking their heads as if Omar had just told them a childish joke.

Omar stared at them, confused. "What's funny?" he asked, his voice hoarse.

One of the officers leaned forward. "Do you really think you were successful in bombing any location?"

Omar's face froze. "What... what do you mean?"

"None of the places you mentioned were attacked," the officer said, still smiling. "Bodh Gaya? Nothing happened. Deoghar? No explosion. Howrah Bridge? Not even a scratch. Same with Kharagpur"

"That's not possible," Omar said, his voice faltering. "I saw the news... the channels were…"

"Those news clips were fake," the man in the suit said calmly. "They were made to deceive you. We knew your team was watching. We fed you what we wanted you to believe."

Omar's breath caught in his throat.

Fake?

Omar sat in the cold interrogation room, his eyes staring blankly at the wall in front of him. The laughter of the officers had long faded, but its echo still rang in his ears. His heart, once full of pride for orchestrating what he believed to be a masterful operation, now beat with a dull thud of shame and disbelief.

The room was silent again. The intelligence officer leaned forward, folded his hands, and began to speak, not with arrogance, but with a calmness that came from knowing the full story.

"Omar," he said, "you and your men were never out of our sight. From the very first day. From the very first meeting. You were under surveillance long before you even crossed the Line of Control."

Omar didn't respond. He couldn't. His throat was dry, and his mind was spinning.

"We deliberately lightened the border security the night you and your team infiltrated. It wasn't a lapse in vigilance but a trap. We wanted you to believe you had slipped in unnoticed."

The officer paused, watching Omar's eyes closely. Then he continued.

"From that moment on, your every step, every call, every meeting was watched. Every location you moved to, every message you passed, we were listening. The only thing you didn't know was that your success was entirely fabricated."

Omar's head tilted slightly, almost involuntarily. The officer saw the crack of disbelief turning into reluctant curiosity.

"You want to know how you saw the news reports of explosions?" the officer said. "How it looked so real, so authentic? Let me walk you through each one."

"In Bodh Gaya, your team kidnapped the family of a local police officer to ensure silence and cooperation. But what you didn't know was that we had already intercepted their location and tapped their calls. We allowed the kidnapping. It was the bait."

"We tracked your team to the officer's house and then to the temple premises. The morning before the bomb was to be planted, we let them proceed. As soon as they planted it and left, our special forces moved in. The bomb was carefully removed and replaced with a harmless replica rigged only for sound and smoke."

"When the moment came, the entire temple complex was sealed discreetly. Tourists were asked to step back, citing an "emergency maintenance operation." Hidden speakers placed around the temple released a low thundering sound, followed by a thick puff of smoke that erupted from behind the prayer platform."

"From a distance, it looked exactly like a blast."

"And the media rushed in with cameras rolling. Seeing the smoke, the army trucks, and the closed premises, they did the rest. They reported it as an explosion."

"You saw those clips and believed you had succeeded."

"Same happened in Howrah. Your men were followed the moment they stepped into Kolkata. From the station to the dingy lodge they stayed in, to the tiny tea stall where they discussed the plan, every location had been bugged."

"When they reached the bridge in the dead of night to plant the explosive under the central section, we let them. They used the narrow side ladder meant for maintenance workers. They thought they were invisible in the night."

"But we were watching."

"As soon as they left the site, the bomb squad moved in. The real bomb was removed, and in its place, we planted a pressure canister filled with thick grey smoke."

"At dawn, the bridge was blocked off. All traffic was halted, officially for "structural inspection." In reality, we were preparing the stage."

"When the timer went off, the smoke rose from the same central section your men had planted their device. Bomb squad vans, soldiers with rifles, and command vehicles moved in with perfect synchronization."

"Again, the media, seeing the activity and the smoke, assumed the worst. Cameras zoomed in. Headlines ran in bold: Terror Blast at Howrah Bridge!"

"Baidhyanath one was the trickiest. The temple received thousands of devotees every single day. Evacuation wasn't an option. Any misstep could cause panic or a stampede."

"Your men were allowed to reach the temple. We watched them from the time they entered Deoghar. Their plan was clever, to use the temple's morning crowd to their advantage and plant the bomb behind one of the donation boxes near the sanctum wall."

"But our men were already inside the temple. Posing as priests, security, and even pilgrims."

"The moment the device was placed, the area around it was quietly sealed using barricades. Without raising alarm, our officers herded the crowd to another wing of the temple, announcing a "VIP visit" requiring restricted access."

"We removed the bomb and sealed the section with a fake blast setup containing smoke machines."

"The blast sound came, the smoke followed, and chaos was contained with pre-positioned CISF and military teams. The media saw it all and concluded - another successful terror attack."

"That's the report you received, Omar."

"Same followed in Kharagpur. Your team's target was the foot overbridge connecting platforms which was crowded, unguarded, and symbolic."

"As soon as you team left the location after giving you a final confirmation, the station was partially locked down. The alternate bridge was kept open. The passengers were informed that a "structural fault" had been detected, and emergency work was underway. The dummy unit with a smoke charge and a timed popper was installed in its place."

"When the blast occurred, smoke filled the stairwell of the footbridge. The army moved in, followed by mock bomb squads in full suits. Media personnel filmed every second broadcasting the news: Explosion at Kharagpur Station!"

"Your men were arrested shortly after making their final calls to you from each location."

"And you?"

"You thought it was confirmation."

"But every single blast you believed in was fake. A carefully designed theatre to make you believe you were winning. In reality, you were walking deeper into the trap."

The officer leaned back in his chair, his eyes fixed on Omar.

"You and your team were fed illusions. Your success was our design. And when your secondary team crossed the border to prepare the final attack at Bagdogra, we closed in."

Omar's face had gone pale.

Everything he had built, every man he trained, every risk he took, was undone by shadows he never saw.

He had believed himself the mastermind of a perfect operation.

But he had merely been a puppet in a larger game, every string pulled by a silent hand he never sensed.

And now, there was nothing left.

Omar sat still, his back slouched against the hard chair. The question had been burning inside him from the moment he regained consciousness in the hospital. With a dry throat and trembling lips, he finally asked, "You could have eliminated us while we crossed the border. Why did you wait for so much to happen?"

The officer across the table leaned back, arms folded, and gave a slow, cunning smile. His eyes didn't blink when he answered.

"Because you weren't the real target, Omar. Zafar was."

The name hit Omar like a slap. Zafar, the elusive, deadly mastermind behind decades of bloodshed. The one man whose words could move sleeper cells across continents. The architect of Omar's mission. The ghost in every operation.

"He was killed," the officer continued calmly. "On the same day you planned the Bagdogra attack."

Omar's breath stopped for a second. "Killed? Zafar…?"

The officer nodded, voice chillingly flat. "Yes. That was the real operation."

For a few seconds, Omar couldn't speak. His thoughts raced back. Zafar had been the one to strategize the multi-location attacks, and had instructed Omar to mobilize the teams. But now he was being told that everything he believed to be his mission was actually designed by the very people he hated.

The officer leaned in, sensing Omar's unraveling mind.

"Zafar had entered India through the Nepal border the night before your Bagdogra mission, to lead the final phase. To take over the Northeast, build camps, set up command centres."

Omar sat, disoriented.

"And we knew. We let the plan grow. We let you think you were winning. Because the day Zafar entered, we were ready."

At a classified location near the Nepal border, Zafar's convoy had been ambushed. Disguised as local herders, the special forces waited silently. As soon as Zafar's jeep crossed the third checkpoint, they surrounded him. A short but fierce exchange of gunfire erupted.

Zafar didn't survive the crossfire.

He was dead before he could even raise his weapon.

The entire mission Omar thought was theirs, was laid out by Indian intelligence to draw out the ghost.

Omar never got an answer to how they made Zafar fall into the trap, how the entire planning done by Zafar was actually planned by the Indian intelligence team and how they made Zafar execute it the way they wanted.

He took that mystery to his grave.

And far away, in the silent fog near the mountains, a lone man in shepherd's clothes, Bashir, kept watching the borders, protecting his motherland in disguise.

Epilogue

For the Brave Who Serve in Silence

This story, though a work of fiction, is rooted in a very real feeling and unshakable depiction of the relentless, tireless, and often invisible efforts of the Indian Defence Forces and Intelligence Agencies who stand as the unseen shield guarding the sovereignty of this nation.

The fall of Omar and the elimination of Zafar was not just a story of one victory. It was a tribute to the spirit of every soldier who walks into danger so that the citizens of India can sleep peacefully at night. It was a silent celebration of every intelligence officer who spends sleepless nights decoding whispers, intercepting shadows, and preventing the next unseen strike before it ever happens.

The mission, as it unfolded, was not a spontaneous act of war. It was a meticulously designed operation that demonstrated not just strength, but sheer brilliance. It was a reflection of the strategic genius, coordination, and precision of the agencies that operate in. Together with the armed forces, these warriors form the backbone of India's national security framework.

While the world saw explosions on the news, it was our intelligence groups who had staged the theatre - fake blasts, controlled evacuations, and subtle manipulations of media narratives. Their goal was not just to prevent terror, but to expose it, dismantle it, and strike at its very heart without letting the enemy know they were already defeated.

From the very moment Omar's team stepped across the border, each movement was watched. Every conversation was intercepted. Every plan he made was shadowed by a counterplan. His confidence, his sense of victory, was carefully fed by our forces, until the moment it all came crashing down.

And yet, the real mission was always Zafar.

He was not just a name, he was a symbol of terror across continents. His death was not by luck or coincidence. It was by design. Years of tracking, informant networks, deep cover operations, and cross-border intelligence cooperation had led to that one perfect moment, when the mastermind believed he was in control, only to find himself surrounded, outplayed, and outgunned.

But such brilliance comes with a cost.

In the silence of the hills near the Nepal border, brave soldiers laid down their lives during the ambush on Zafar's convoy. They did not return to a hero's welcome. Their names were never spoken on primetime news. They became the stories whispered in army canteens, remembered in memorial walls, and etched forever in the hearts of their comrades.

This story is for them.

For the men who knew the enemy would shoot first, but still chose to walk ahead.

For the ones who died without a name, so that millions could live without fear.

And for the ones who continue to stand watch, unseen, unheard, but always there.

India's intelligence community is not just about spies and codes. It is a network of minds, trained to see what others overlook. It is a system built on the shoulders of analysts, linguists, tech experts, cyber warriors, and field agents. It is a force that adapts every day - evolving to meet threats that change form, shape, and geography.

Be it a message intercepted from a border radio, a suspicious transfer of money flagged by a bank, or a sudden shift in satellite data, each clue becomes part of a larger puzzle. And somewhere in a dark room, an officer connects the dots before anyone even realizes there's a pattern forming.

These heroes wear no medals. They fight without fanfare. Their victories are never paraded. And yet, their every success writes a new chapter of peace for this country.

Let us not forget the Indian Armed Forces—Army, Navy, Air Force, paramilitary forces, and the special task units. Their discipline, courage, and sharp coordination with the intelligence units make operations like the one that stopped Omar and Zafar possible.

Let us also remember the unsung villagers, the local informants, the ordinary citizens who share a suspicion, pass a note, or alert a constable, without realizing that they just helped save lives.

*National security is not just the job of uniformed men and women. It is a collective consciousness—**a shared duty**.*

This book, in its small way, is a salute to every such hand that holds the line of defence. To every silent warrior in the shadows. To every mother who sends her son to the border with pride in her eyes and fear in her heart. To every father who salutes the flag and hides the tears when the tricolor is handed to him folded.

It is a tribute to the martyrs—those who never came back. And to the living heroes—those who continue to fight, knowing they may never be remembered.

In a time where terror evolves every minute, and threats no longer wear uniforms, our protectors must stay ten steps ahead. And they do. With intelligence that surpasses borders. With courage that doesn't flinch. With a sense of duty that never tires.

The story of Omar, Zafar, and the shadows that surround them is just a reminder of the real game being played every day, where the stakes are not points, but lives. Where the enemies may never show their faces, but the protectors never turn theirs away.

So, the next time we walk freely through a market, pray peacefully at a temple, board a train without fear, or watch the national flag flutter in the wind—we must remember, someone, somewhere, stood watch to make that moment possible.

And to them, we owe not just our gratitude, but our unwavering respect.

Jai Hind.

Dedication

To the Silent Sentinels of Our Nation—

This book is dedicated to the brave men and women of the Indian Defence Forces, Intelligence Agencies, and Special Forces who protect our motherland with unwavering courage, unmatched intelligence, and quiet sacrifice.

To those who serve in uniform, and to those who serve in the shadows.

To those who come back with medals, and to those who return draped in the tricolor.

To the families who wait, and the ones who weep.

This story is a tribute to your honor.

You are the reason we sleep peacefully.

You are the reason our flag flies high.

You are the true heroes of this land.

Jai Hind.

Author's Note

When I first set out to write this story, it was simply an idea, one that merged imagination with inspiration. But as the pages unfolded, it became something deeper. A mirror to the hidden battles our nation's protectors fights every day, often unnoticed and unsung.

This book is fiction. But the essence of it, the sharp intelligence, the strategic brilliance, the relentless pursuit of safety, and the silent sacrifices, is very real.

India is not just guarded by guns and uniforms. It is guarded by minds that stay awake while the world sleeps. This is my small attempt to honor those minds. The analysts, the field agents, the operatives, the soldiers, and the commanders, each one of them is a pillar in the temple of national security.

To every soul who fights for this country, in boardrooms and bunkers, in deserts and data centres, I offer my deepest respect.

And to the readers, may this story remind us of the price of peace, and the worth of those who ensure it.

With reverence,

— *Abhishek Kumar*

Also by the author...

Read about the story of passion, commitment, challenges, overcoming fears, sacrifices and many more.

Deepali represents each woman who ever had dream of following her passion, but was pushed to family commitments and she fights till the end for a better future.

www.ingramcontent.com/pod-product-compliance
Lightning Source LLC
Chambersburg PA
CBHW060530160726
47991CB00001B/255